Telham Park novels by
Jennifer Burton:

Princess' Journey

Christopher's Dilemma

Kenya's Song

Brian's Connection

Telham Park

BRIAN'S CONNECTION

JENNIFER BURTON

ALEXZUS BOOKS

New York

ALEXZUS Books
244 Fifth Avenue
Suite B260
New York, NY 10001

The characters and events in this book are fictitious. Any similarity to real persons, living or dead, is coincidental and not intended by the author.

Cover design by Rick Turylo

ISBN 978-0-9724733-5-4

Library of Congress number 2011909033

Printed in the United States of America

February 2012

For Malcom Craig

one

T he crowded subway train had inched at such a snail's pace, Brian Parker didn't realize it had stopped. Immersed in his videocam, he viewed the footage of Chang, Malyck, and David taken at Crampton's Computer Camp (CCC) this past summer. Brian's cackling in the sudden quiet drew peculiar looks from those near him but he didn't care. Viewing the pictures brought back memories of a carefree existence away from parents and overbearing rules. Well . . . not all rules.

Look at you, Chang. The Chinese native worked intensely at his laptop wearing an Afro wig he referred to as his 'inspiration.' Now living in Connecticut, he could rap with the style of a homegrown urbanite—syntax, gestures, and all. At 5'4", the virtual programming apprentice amused his friends with his eloquent tongue.

Malyck, a resident of Nyack, New York, had come from India just two years before. Dark, handsome, and disciplined to a fault, he worked ceaselessly in spite of the onset of Parkinson's disease. He was rarely caught without that beaming smile, and behind it came nothing but brilliance. The four depended on him when the technology became unusually complicated. *Ah, the future tech evangelist.* That's what they called him.

Sailing down the slippery slopes of Sweden Mountains during winter breaks was David, a.k.a. Rekcah—or 'hacker' spelled backward. Only sixteen—as they all were—Rekcah's German and Swedish parents moved to the United States and settled in New Jersey where he was born. They called him the global broker, as he imparted his big ideas about connecting third-world nations through technological development—all while entertaining them with the D-2000 acoustic guitar. He had a descent voice, too. There they were, all singing the lyrics to *Counterfeit Planet*, one of Rekcah's contagious originals.

Brian reversed the video and watched it a second time, anticipating the plans they had for the coming year. Already well into the third week of spring, summer beckoned and it would soon be time for camp again. Throughout the year IV4 (Integrated Vision Four) got together for lunch at the Battle Rock Café in Manhattan's Times Square on the second Saturday of every month. That's where he was coming from.

In the blink of an eye the train suddenly went black. Darkness halted all movement and the simple chatter of commuting passengers ceased. The engine rumbled to a crescendo and then shut off. A delay was inevitable, the only question in everyone's mind was how long.

Ironically, Brian recalled how the lights went out the same way at camp last year in the bite of a tempestuous thunderstorm. The atmospheric discharge of lightning bolts streaking through the Catskills in upstate New York could be quite severe. Just like that, the light switched to darkness. The emotions of twenty-two wired students flared at once, with the single fear of losing their information.

When the light returned, several passengers walked through the car moving toward the front of the train. Last in line was the conductor, who stopped inside the car and allowed the rolling door to snap shut behind him.

"Are we're going to be delayed long?" Brian asked.

"Doubt it . . . but I'll get the word in a minute." His voice was bigger than one would expect for an average-sized black man who appeared to be somewhere in his thirties.

Viewing more recent footage of friends, fishing in the fall with his dad, in concert with Rapper Elo-Quince, and an ex-homeless 17-year-old artist designing T-shirts by hand in Telham Park, revived his present. Speaking of sales, he remembered the possible iPad trade and reached for his phone to check his messages. More silence followed by a 'Call failed' response was what he received instead. Underground with no communication, he thought, looking up and catching the eye of the conductor.

"You always work this line?" Brian asked the man out of boredom, who's sluggish demeanor looked like he'd rather be elsewhere.

His reply led to a recall of his past schedules and onto future aspirations. Though the two had just met, they conversed like old acquaintances. Brian had a certain way about him that made people feel very comfortable. He could quiet a crying baby or engage in a spirited conversation with a politician—just like that.

"Ay, so what do think about that new train? The way they designed the seats is kinda—"

"Smoke up ahead," the motorman radioed to the conductor. "I can see the flames."

"What's it lookin' like?" asked the conductor.

"Ah . . . it appears to be a fire on the track. Come up and take a look."

"Duty calls, man," said the conductor, extending his hand to Brian for a firm shake. "Stay strong."

"Alright."

The conductor's ring of keys jingled to the rhythm of his stride as he walked through the car. Minutes later, Brian walked to the front of the train to see what was happening. The crowd stalled his movement in the first car and his gaze rested on a familiar young woman depositing a book into her denim backpack. Observing her highlighted satiny twists draped across her cinnabar skin, he imagined she was a cross between an African American, Indian or a South American. Tossing glances, she looked curious about the ensuing dilemma and maybe a little anxious too as a smoky stench filled the car.

"Good afternoon, ladies and gentlemen, please excuse the interruption," said a rheumy eyed, African American whose face and tattered clothing portrayed a troubled past. The foul stench of his body permeated the smell of smoke as he squeezed between the passengers. "I represent the Zale House, a shelter for homeless families that, due to unfortunate circumstances, have found themselves with no income and nowhere to—"

His words seemed to fade as Brian's gaze returned to the young girl, who darted her sensual eyes over the stranger fishing for change. He reached into his pocket and absently handed all his change to the solicitor as he passed by.

"God bless," he mumbled thankfully.

"The station's on fire!" an older gentleman said, and the lights suddenly shut off again.

"There could be terrorists!" a woman voiced above the quiet hush.

Brian caught a glimpse of flames shooting out from the station ahead but didn't panic. He gauged the distance of the train's position. *The motorman's gonna have to move the train and align the first set of doors with the platform for a safe exit.*

"Attention all passengers," the conductor announced. "Attention all passengers. Due to a fire on the tracks up ahead, this will be the last stop. I repeat. Due to a fire on the tracks in the station ahead, this will be the last stop. All passengers must exit the train from the first car."

The train jerked suddenly and slowly inched forward to the platform just as Brian had thought. Relieved of ensuing danger, he studied the girls' every move.

I could slide up on her with some conversation. Or maybe take a ride with her . . . anywhere, doesn't matter.

OR I could offer her something to eat—even though I'm not hungry right now—or better yet, stop in Coffee Capital for some cappuccino.

When the doors opened hordes of people crowded between them and she was soon swept away out of his sight. Brian moved through the exit turnstile upstairs and into the bright light of the spring day. He vigorously scanned the still faces and passersby alike, but there was no sign of her. On instinct, he changed direction and walked toward another subway line, only four blocks away. The shrill whistle from a man hailing a cab directed his attention to the other side of the street. In that fleeting moment he spotted the denim backpack moving through throngs of people.

"Excuse me. Oh, sorry. Excuse me," he uttered and dashed across the street, not leaving a single chance to lose her. Moving quickly, he ignored the sea of strange faces swimming toward him and walked into two elderly white women, almost knocking one over.

"My heavens!" one of them railed back, frightened. "What in the world—"

"Oooh, I'm sorry," Brian apologized, extending his hand to help her.

She eyed him indignantly before gauging his sincerity.

The other woman was taller and less fragile, hair as white as a sheep with unforgiving eyes. "What were ya thinkin'?"

"I . . . I was in a hurry," Brain stammered. "Tryin' to catch my bus. I'm sorry."

"Haste, young man . . . doesn't pay," the smaller one said.

"Yes, yes, I know. I'm sorry, okay?"

Brian imagined what those two ladies really wanted to say to him, but there was little to come back with since a genuine apology had been offered. He continued to walk, but now she was out of sight.

At the corner intersection he slowed down as the crowds had thinned out. To the east he saw her, admiring her proud stride and shapely physique. Had he gone crazy, following a young woman he didn't even know?

When she turned into Delmar's Fruit Market Delicatessen, he perused the section of snacks, and grabbed a pack of pistachios to purchase. He watched her hand the woman, who spoke with authority like she could have been the owner, a piece of paper, but couldn't make sense of their dialogue.

Walking into the pharmacy a few doors down, it was a repeat of the same. Entering the nail salon, the cleaners, and a beauty supply store he watched her handing the clerk a piece of paper, speak a few words, and she was out.

Maybe she's selling something 'cause she can't possibly live over here.

The next few blocks were becoming more residential. Businesses and restaurants were storefronts of two-and three-story apartment buildings. She came up upon an old, gray-stoned church with narrow stained glass windows surrounded by an eroding black fence and made her way through the long line of downtrodden looking men waiting to get inside.

"What can I do for you?" asked a husky, bearded white man who stopped Brian at the door.

"Ah . . . I want to speak to the young lady."

"What young lady?"

"She just walked in. Um, Serena."

"Who?"

"Serena."

"There's nobody workin' here by that name," he replied, looking skeptical. Then he pointed Brian toward the back of the line.

Keeping the space between the line tight, white, black, and Hispanic men guarded their positions making it impossible to jump ahead.

"You got the time?" Brian asked the white man who was last on line.

The man pointed his trembling finger to the top of a building some distance away. Squinting, he read the clock. "Uh . . . ten to four."

"How long do you think it's gonna be before we get in?" Brian asked.

"Forty minutes to an hour," he shrugged stretching a grin. "If it's moving. Food came in late today." The man's teeth were dark yellow and green. Underneath the knit hat, his face was sunken down to his jawbones. "I heard they got hot pastrami."

When the line moved inside he followed the men downstairs to a large, stark basement, where the men received their food—hot soup and a sandwich— on cardboard trays. He waited the better part of an hour, conversed with a few of them in the hopes of seeing her appear again. But she never did.

THE VISION of her exquisite face burned in Brian's mind as he approached Jeremy's Clean Cut Barbershop in Telham Park. The second level of the three-story brownstone was a social lounge, where men—young and old—collaborated with honest exchange.

It was crowded and lively inside the small, brightly lit space where men kicked back in the sleek leather seating watching the *Thriller* music video on the flat screen TV.

"What up, family?" Brian hailed, cutting through the noise and heading toward Country, his preferred barber.

Malachi and Malcolm slid across the gleaming black granite mimicking the zombies in the choreographed dance routine shifting, shaking and popping, prompting a loud applause.

Unfazed by the ruckus, Country clipped the customer's head with great precision. His uncle had owned Jeremy's shop for over twenty years, and he visited Telham Park during the summer months to help him work. Since he graduated from high school more than two years before, he decided to forego college and become a full time barber. At twenty years of age he had ambitions to open a chain of high tech unisex salons. His deep Southern accent was borne out of the cornfields of Alabama, thus landing Sheldon Jettersby his nickname.

"Country!"

"Master tech," he replied, twirling a toothpick in his mouth.

"Whatchu been up to?"

"Makin' it do what it do."

"I see ya work. Lookin' good."

"Whatchu gettin'?"

"I don't know. Whatchu think?" Brian asked, observing his kinky bush of hair in the mirror. It was thick and uneven.

"Cut it off," Country replied, his eyes glued to the young man's head. "Thing look like a rug."

"Watch yourself, dude. Ay . . . give me a dark Caesar? Yeah, that's what I need."

Observing his profile, then his face, Brian's dark, deep-set eyes looked back at him. *Does my stocky build look appealing? Or, do I look like an overweight, lazy marshmallow-type dude whose had one fast food meal too many?*

Country shot a glance over at Brian and chuckled. "Look like somebody been smitten."

"Go 'head man."

"She look good?"

"Psss . . . baddest girl I ever seen."

"I'm tellin' ya. Clean look . . . she'll be eatin' out ya palms. Unless she's one of them wild types, like it real nappy so she can dangle from the ends of it."

"I don't know about that," Brian blushed. His eyes then fell on Christopher who had raised his head out of the book he was reading. "Playa, playa, I didn't see you, man. What up?"

"Everything's good," Christopher responded, closing his book. Though he was more popularly known as the Telham Park High School track star, the people closest to him admired his affinity for history and knew he was a voracious reader.

"What's going on with the Princess?"

Everyone associated Christopher and Princess as a couple, though technically they were only friends.

"She's good, good. Came home for the ceremony last week at the African Burial Ground in Manhattan."

"Don't tell me I missed it."

"Yo . . . it was—"

"Everybody was there," Malachi jumped in, stepping up to one of the other's barber's chair. "Politicians. Celebrities. Rappaz."

"Ah man," Brian scowled. " 'Cause I had heard about it, yo. Then I got busy . . . forgot all about it."

"Zori showed up," said Christopher. "He performed in the afternoon."

"Word!"

"He rocked 'em," praised Malcolm.

"All of them did," said Malachi. "But that anthropologist, Gossett . . . he took us some place we never been. Yo, we were—"

"Skeletons of women with their babies," interjected Tim, opening his eyes. Country was lining the arch around his ear. "I saw some dudes gettin' emotional up in there."

"I was feeling it, too," Christopher said. "If the skeletons of the slaves don't wake you up—"

"Remember the picture of the 38-year-old dude?" asked Country. "He looked like an old man."

"The stress of that labor was killin' 'em," commented Tim.

"You were there, Country?" Brian was surprised.

"I had to be."

"Yo . . . I'm gonna be there next year . . . for real."

As Country removed the cape from Tim, Christopher stood up and reached in his pocket for money.

"You breakin' out?" Brian asked.

"In a minute," Christopher replied, pointing his head toward Joshua, his little brother, who was in one of the barber's chairs toward the back.

"Li'l Chris. Lookin' just like you, man."

"Yeah, I know."

"I see you got him readin', too."

"Each one gotta teach one," said Christopher reaching for his book.

"That's whassup."

"What's that you got there?" asked Kyle, a.k.a. the 'Crusada', the devoted Christian.

"Politics Behind the Movement, yo, with Martin Luther's King. This man is—"

"Heavy, ain't he?" said a young man named Quinton.

"When I read this stuff, yo . . . I got to pause and reflect. 'Cause check this out, can you believe he . . . this one little dude . . . carried the civil rights movement from the South into the North? No map, no plan, just one step ahead of the next bomb."

"And a lot of those cats following them were young," Kyle added eagerly. "Like us . . . sixteen, maybe—"

"Goes to show you the power of one man," Quinton broke in.

"We don't know nothin' about that today," a heavyset guy named Mark said.

"Nah, everything was *urgent* with them," said Payton, another patron. "They were determined to get theirs."

"But you know, I think he knew his time was gonna be short so they had to get results—quick," Roger Morton, a twenty-something man seated on the other side of Kyle offered.

"You hit the nail right on the head with dat dare," said Country.

His response piqued Kyle's interest. "Whatchu know about Martin?"

"Huh . . . when they were securing the voting rights for the people in Selma, my granddaddy was right there wid 'em."

"Word?" Christopher remarked, intrigued by the connection.

"Went to jail two, three, fo' times."

Payton was surprised. "What was your grandfather into?"

Country paused and turned his customer's chair around to outline the left side of his head. "Farming . . . owned some land."

"That was good for that time," said a tall, thin dude who lived in the next town over, but came to get his hair cut every Saturday at Jeremy's. His name was Gregg.

"But they didn't care about none of that," said Payton. "Those dudes were ready to die for the cause."

"They had the faith," Kyle added, "and the muscle in numbers."

"That's right," agreed Country. "And what they show you on television . . . that's a bunch of glamour. Stories my granddaddy use to tell me . . . give you the chills."

"Videos, DVDs, computer games," Michael Dodson announced entering the shop.

"Big Mike," Brian called out, extending his hand to view the merchandise. "My man, whatchu askin' for these?"

"Ten and Fifteen. But for you," he said, stretching his eyes comically. "Give me ten."

"This one's good?"

"Hard-core, yo. Can't get enough of 'em."

Brian bought the video game, thought on some more and purchased another one. Money began exchanging hands like water. Soon after, Country swiveled Brian around to see himself in the mirror. "Aiight, Master Tech."

The finished haircut punctuated his features; edges evened to precision made him easy to look at.

"Cool," he approved, handing Country thirteen dollars.

"Keep hope alive," Brian said, shaking hands with his people and headed home.

two

"That's not the same one you had before," Brian said, eyeballing Ricky's iPod. They were eating at his best friend's favorite table in the back of McCuller's Restaurant on Monday, giving them a clear visual of the girls coming in and out of the restroom.

"Nope," replied Ricky, glancing at what he referred to as the rear assets of a popular junior named Sierra as she passed by. "I got this one from work. Maxicomm's one of my company's client."

"You get all the perks at that job," noted Brian, pulling discriminately from a mountain of cheese fries.

"Right on time, 'cause the battery in my old one ran out. Then I was going to have to pay for a new one, and that takes time 'cause you gotta send it away and that takes three to four weeks and all they gonna do is—"

"Just bring me a new battery," Brian said. "I know how to change it."

"Cool," replied Ricky, his nickname for Ricardo. He was the Hispanic version of Brian. The pudgy type and cute, only he wore glasses. Could stand to loose a pound or two or twenty, but he carried himself like a lightweight. Inserting his earphones he rocked to the beat of the music. "I downloaded all the Bikko joints . . . the new one, too."

Brian was somewhere else now, lost in a sleepy illusion.

"You in a daze, yo."

"No I'm not," Brian said, coming back alive. "I was tryin' to put something together in my mind."

"Like what, you and her?"

"Stop that," grinned Brian, picking up a fry and biting off the tip.

"Yeah, that's what you're doin'," Ricky declared, placing the lettuce and tomatoes between his burger. "I can't believe you followed her like that."

"That's what I did."

Ricky started laughing.

"What's so funny?" Brian asked, resisting the temptation to join him.

"Ay . . . I should've known something was up when you shaved that head."

Brian shifted forward with a gleam in his eye. "But you had to see her, I'm serious. She was like a bronze goddess, yo . . . without the accoutrement."

"Without the *what*?" Ricky frowned awkwardly biting into his burger.

"Her face was like . . . sunshine. Even without the hair she would still be a honey."

"She don't have any hair?" Ricky asked.

"Picture that. She has a head full of hair, yo, but I'm sayin' . . . I could see her essence . . . she just radiated . . . follow me? That's what accoutrement means. I got that from my father."

"Okay, now you're gettin' poetic on me. But I don't understand how you let her get away?"

"I didn't," Brian said, pulling at the lip of his cap. "I thought she was gonna come back outside."

"That's crazy, yo."

"And once I got in, I still didn't see her," Brian explained, shifting his hat from side to side. "If I was thinking I could have taken a picture."

"How you gonna find her?" Ricky asked, adjusting his glasses on the bridge of his nose.

"*You* gonna find her."

"Me?"

"Yeah."

"But you're not giving me nothin'."

"You work for lawyers. They can find anybody."

"They're not investigators. They do bankruptcies and wills . . . stuff like that. And you don't even know the address."

"I didn't see any numbers."

"If you at least had the name of the church we could find it and see what's going on in there."

"That's true . . . but whatever she's doing may not have anything to do with the church," said Brian. "It might be some kind of organization using the church, like how they use Cornerstone Baptist for that 'One Nation' program."

"But who knows, it may have been a one day thing going on, which means you would still need the church information to follow up on it."

Brian lifted the lip of his cap, scratched his head, and lowered it again. "I gotta find this girl, yo."

"Watch yourself, they're trouble. You heard about Solomar?"

"Nah, what's goin' on with him?"

"Remember the girl he was with . . . dark, real pretty?"

"You talkin' about um . . . um, I think her name is Crystal?"

"Yeah. She's having another baby."

"Wait a minute," Brian halted, looking bug-eyed. "When did she have the first one?"

"When she was fifteen . . . and that one's not Solomar's. Her mother's raising the kid. Now she's pregnant with his baby."

"That's rough, yo," Brian remarked. "I feel for him."

"My brother got messed up like that."

"I thought Orlando wanted a kid."

"That's what he *thought* he wanted 'cause he was so in love with his girl. But all that changed when little Poppy was born. That's my heart and we love him to death, but my brother tells me all the time . . . don't do it!"

"I hear dat."

"I don't know . . . the way you're talking, you already in love."

"Nah, man. I just want to find her," Brian said depositing one last French fry in his mouth and slapped a ten dollar bill on the table. "I'ma go check out that new 3D PSP."

"I gotchu next time."

"Cool."

THE NUT factory on Braddock Street was about to close that evening and Brian made it in only seconds before the manager locked the doors. He wasn't as lucky catching the bus home as it quickly cornered the block and kept moving without him. Walking, thoughts of a new PSP version excited him as he snacked on a bag of raw cashews. *With taxes and everything, you're looking at close to three hundred. I can probably get Ma to help me out. Forget Dad. But I might have enough to get it without either of them knowing. Nah, then I'll have to answer a thousand questions.*

Arriving home, Brian stopped cold when he was met by two unknown white men standing in his living room, and the troubled look on his father's face.

"What's going on, Dad?"

"Would this be Brian?" The older one asked. He was thick and muscular, dark featured and middle-aged.

"Yes," Mr. Parker nodded.

Brian could feel his heart thumping, hoping not to hear any bad news. "Something happened? Where's Ma?"

"Your mother's fine. This is Detective Wallace," Mr. Parker said, introducing the younger one first. He was taller, clean-cut with brown hair. "And this is Detective Conyers. They want to ask you some questions."

"Ask *me* some questions . . . about what?" A familiar, uneasy feeling invaded him. The same one he felt when his father harshly intercepted his plans that he and some friends had to hack into the cellular phone account of a celebrity so one of the friends' brother could access her address and make a move on her. It was later discovered to be a covert plan to rob the woman and Brian had been taken for a fool. The impatient gleam in his father's eyes rattled Brian's insides.

"You know someone by the name of Thomas or Tommy Manicello?" asked Detective Conyers.

Caught off-guard, he couldn't immediately recall. "I...I don't know anybody—"

"A white guy, taller than you, dark hair," Detective Wallace interjected. Though his voice was commanding and authoritative, he had an easygoing manner.

Brian frowned, pulling together his mental roster of associates. He thought of someone he knew who fit that description, but that wasn't his name. "Doesn't sound familiar," he said nodding slowly.

"Sure you don't know this guy?" asked Detective Conyers, his cold, gray eyes trained uncomfortably on him.

"Nah . . . I mean no."

"Know anybody by that name online?" asked Detective Wallace.

Brian's eyes darted quickly over at his father and then to the detectives.

"I don't know. Maybe—"

"You just said you didn't know him," Mr. Parker said sternly. "But that look on your face is saying different. Which one is it?"

"I don't know that name."

"This says you do," countered Detective Wallace, presenting a printout corroborating their email communication. "Calls himself 'Eye On The Game Zuloo'."

"So what's up?" Detective Conyers probed. "I see some communication between the two of you. Friday, the 17th, Wednesday the 22nd—"

"Wait a minute," Brian said, recognizing his email signature. "That's T-Man."

"And where do you know this guy from?" Mr. Parker asked, fidgeting with the coins inside his pocket.

"One of my friends introduced me . . . at school."

"And what are y'all talking about?"

"He had some questions about filming on the Web."

"What kind of films?" Detective Wallace asked.

"I don't know," Brian shrugged. "Never said anything about them." He looked over at his father, whose eyes were boring into him. "And I never asked."

"And what do you know about making films?" Detective Wallace surveyed him closely.

Brian glanced at his father, uncertain how to respond.

"He knows a little something about computers," Mr. Parker explained. "We send him to summer camps and all of that."

"He didn't give you any indication about the kinds of films or videos he was making?" asked Detective Wallace.

"No. He just wanted some information on streaming, doing some live stuff. I turned him on to a couple of programs 'cause my friend said he needed—"

"How long have you known Christina?" Detective Conyers broke in, drawing up a lopsided smile.

"Who?" Brian grimaced. "I don't know anyone named Christina."

Detective Conyers smothered a heavy cough, glancing over at the other. "How often do you visit this guy?"

"Visit him? Never happened. I told you we just hit each other back and forth online."

"How long has he been filming porn?" he asked, turning quickly to suppress another cough.

Brian glanced from one detective to the next and then to his father in blank astonishment. "What?"

"You know anything about that?" Mr. Parker asked, his eyes cutting and threatening.

"Pornography? No!"

Clearing his throat, Detective Conyers asked, "So you're saying you don't have any knowledge about Down Below Cinema?"

"Somebody saw you there," accused Detective Wallace.

"Saw me where?" Brian jerked his head back, bewildered. "I don't even know where this guy lives."

"He's running a porn studio out of his basement at home," Conyers revealed.

Brian was baffled. "You're jokin', right?"

"Nothin' funny here," Detective Wallace said. "He's using underaged girls to sell pornography . . . live and in color."

"And he's got a special deal for first-time customers," added Detective Conyers.

Detective Wallace looked puzzled. "So what did you think he was doing when he was asking you questions about making films?"

"I didn't think anything. People make short films or videos all the time."

"You ever made movies before?"

"Uh . . . yeah. I've filmed some things . . . but all my friends—"

"What kind of things?" Detective Conyers interjected.

Brian hunched his shoulders thinking. "Little things . . . like I might film a trip or a party. Sometimes I film properties for my mother to show her clients. You want to see 'em?"

The two detectives exchanged glances, nodded affirmatively. "That's not necessary," Detective Conyers said. They appeared satisfied. "That's all for now."

"Let me talk to these men," Mr. Parker told Brian, pointing his head toward the stairs.

Brian couldn't make it to his room fast enough. He cleared the heap of clothes piled on his chair, collected the magazines strewn about the room, and plopped down on his bed. Unable to sit still, he turned on his music, programmed to his favorite iTunes, checked his email, and turned on the video game.

Later, when Brian felt the thumping vibration of his father's footsteps coming up the stairs, he turned off the game and picked up the closest book he could find. He could hear him explaining what had happened to his mother, who had apparently just come home.

"You've got detectives coming to my house," Mr. Parker said, bolting through the door. He had removed his shirt and tie, and the fitted T-shirt he wore revealed his broad, muscular chest.

"I didn't know they were coming here."

"What's going on, Brian?" Mrs. Parker asked. He had inherited his mother's features, the same biscuit-brown complexion, chestnut eyes, and pleasingly plump lips.

"Nothin', Ma."

"Preparing for your new career as a cyber crook?" The voice of the six-foot-three, disciplinarian growled when he was angry. "Got a scheme for everything. America's dumbest criminal, that's what we need to cast you for."

"But I'm not guilty of anything!"

"Tell us the truth," urged Mrs. Parker. "Why did those men come here?"

"They were askin' me questions about this dude I met from one of my friends at school. I was helping him with some webcasting, that's all."

"You so quick to get involved with people," Mr. Parker admonished. "What did I tell you about that? You're not from the streets and you don't know the game! That's why you're always getting caught!"

"But I met the dude one time."

"And that should've been enough," he said, looking over Brian's room and found his video case. "See, this is what I mean."

"Oh my God," Brian whined.

Mrs. Parker ran her hand through her lengthy hair and dropped her shoulders impatiently. "Didn't your father tell you not to buy those violent video games?"

"It's no big deal, Ma. Why he beastin'?"

"What!"

Brian backed away hastily, out of his father's reach.

"You're spending *my* money on this trash when I told you *not* to bring this violence in my house."

By now Brian was backed into the corner—resentful and fearful at the same time. *He's fuming and getting ready to blow. What's he gonna do now?*

"You don't have enough work to do?" he asked, scanning the room. "Where's your books?"

"Over there," Brian pointed. "I'm getting ready to do my homework."

"You think I'm stupid?" asked Mr. Parker who lunged at Brian.

"Calvin, no!" piped Mrs. Parker, pulling him back. "We're not going there."

"I'm always asking you about school. What classes you're taking? How are your grades looking? I get a grunt here, a shrug there." Mr. Parker tossed a glance at his wife. "I think he's crazy."

"Stop saying that! He's just got sixteen-year-old issues!"

Brian looked away fuming, and then turned back and scowled. He wanted so badly to stand up to his father, he could taste it.

"You got a problem?" Mr. Parker asked, catching the look. "Too many rules for you?"

Brian stood still, eyeballing his father and then turned away mumbling. "If you were all that interested you would come up to my school and see—"

"What was that?"

". . . I'm saying Dad, you're always working. You don't have the time to come to school like Ma. Then the first thing you wanna—"

"I'm working all day trying to build something for this family. Where do you think all of this comes from?"

"Calvin, stop it! His mother persisted. "All of this over a video game."

"It's not the video, it's the *principle*. Then again, it is the video. How much you paid for this . . . twenty, thirty dollars?"

"Ten."

"It's only ten dollars, Calvin. We got bigger things to—"

"Like ten dollars is nothing," he raged. "Go out there and make ten dollars since it's so easy. When you get a job and live in the house that *you're* paying the mortgage on, you can spend your money any way you like, but not here."

Mr. Parker rummaged through the game vault and began inspecting the titles. "I'm taking these out of here."

"Why, Dad?"

"Keep your mouth closed," his mother warned.

He confiscated his laptop, iPod, Xbox, his MP3 player, his portable DVD, and his Blackberry. Returning to Brian's room Mr. Parker snatched the wires out of his television and cable box and rolled them up.

"You're takin' my television, too?"

"You mean *my* television. And what are you gonna do about it?"

Brian turned away, exasperated.

"We bust our butts everyday so you can have not only everything you need, but the things you want," Mr. Parker said. "And this is what we get. Especially when it's evident that you can't hold a job. Your last attempt at work got you mixed up in some conspiracy to take a New York City train. Who ever heard of—"

"It wasn't like we were planning to steal the train. It was a bet to see who could—"

"What!" Mr. Parker turned swiftly toward him, cutting him off. "Open your mouth when I'm speakin' again and you'll be—"

"Don't do it!" insisted Mrs. Parker, stepping in between them.

"That's the problem. You can't tell him anything. On top of that he's selfish. Lazy. Look at this room. He's a pig!"

"Enough, Calvin!"

"And you're part of the problem," he said, walking out the door and then returned to the room. "Giving, giving, giving him all the time. He's never gonna learn—"

"Don't take me there," admonished Mrs. Parker.

"And you're not allowed to leave this house," commanded Mr. Parker, "other than to go to school and to run errands. That's until further notice!" He looked around the room one final time mumbling before exiting. "I'm not one of your friends' parents. Wanna do what *you* want to do? Go live with them!"

When his Mrs. Parker left the room, Brian slid down into his chair staring at an empty desk. Feeling defeated and misunderstood, he wanted to drive his fist through the wall. *Whose father gets twisted over video games? What world is he living in? Cave dweller!*

The dissension between Brian and Mr. Parker was nothing new. In earlier years, Mr. Parker's military career had required then to move to several cities around the world. On deployment most of the time, Mr. Parker's relationship with Brian developed intermittently. When his military career ended, it brought the family a welcomed sense of stability, though Mr. Parker couldn't seem to part with his regimented lifestyle. He was hard on Brian, ruling the house like a boot camp. After all, as the son of a retired Air Force Captain turned investment banker, Brian was supposed to excel in every endeavor. But as time progressed, he didn't meet his father's expectations, and they couldn't see eye to eye on anything.

Twenty minutes had passed, and Brian could hear his parents arguing in their bedroom. Frustrated, he began to gather his clothes, putting them neatly in their proper places. He reached over to turn on his CD player and suddenly remembered it wasn't there. Nor his iPod or MP3 player.

Just like his room, his closet was a disorganized mess. Underneath a pile of clothes he discovered his old playstation. *Ahhh, he didn't get everything.* Then he remembered there was an old television in the garage that worked. Glancing wildly around the room, he searched for a place to hide it when the door suddenly flew open.

"You found another toy," Mr. Parker sneered. "Hand it over," he demanded, and snatched it out of his hand. "You won't be getting any allowance from me *or* your mother for the next two weeks, understand?"

Brian showed no reaction.

"You heard me?"

"I heard you," Brian replied dryly.

The door slammed, crushing Brian's hopes for salvaging some part of his livelihood. *This dude is crazy! Treatin' me like a child. I'm a grown man.* Exasperated, he kicked the leg of his desk, causing his books to topple off, and then composed himself. He solemnly picked them up one by one deciding on which one to read. After all, he had nothing else to do.

three

Just minutes past midnight, the waning crescent moon was barely visible beneath the veil of cloudy obscurity. Lying in bed, fully awake and discomforted, Brian's mind raced. His stomach growled in protest, wanting more than the few cashews he had tossed down earlier, since he had refused to face his parents and eat dinner with them. *It was only a video game. I know he screamed about it more than ten times, but Dude. . . .*

The streetlight cast a thin screen of light on the wall facing him. Becoming his imaginary computer monitor, he searched the Web in his mind. Out of the blue, music began to play; fleeting images of movies, videos, and virtual games ran rampant in his head.

Outside, a birdcall twitter bleeped twice and deactivated a car alarm. A door slammed shut. Then the ignition choked and slid into power. In the heavy silence Brian's sense of hearing seemed annoyingly sensitive.

Inescapably restless, he launched up from his bed, carefully tiptoeing in the dark past his parents' room and down the stairs. The open blinds in the kitchen illuminated a path to the basement. But first he was drawn toward the gleaming clock of the microwave and snuck a peek into the refrigerator. He took several slices of provolone cheese and half the package of turkey breast and stuffed it his mouth.

The soft carpeting in the quiet basement felt like a walk in the sand. Brian eased his way to his mother's desk, sat down, and logged onto the Internet. His parents were smiling with a giant waterscape behind them in the leather-framed portrait. It had been taken in Atlantis, Bahamas. The memory of the tropical paradise brought a smile to his lips as he looked with pride at their youthful appearances. No one ever guessed they were in their forties.

As he checked his email, Brian reached inside the desk drawer and grabbed a couple of Granola bars. But soon his mind wandered playing Solitaire and Masteroids. Before he knew it, an entire hour had passed, and two more Granola bars were gone.

His thoughts returned to the girl, and he Googled a search for churches in Manhattan. When the Yellow Page directory came up, he wrote down the names and addresses of churches in the area, and then clicked on the "One Time Chance" chat room.

YEMI402: What is the temperature in America?

Brian saw that there were only three of them in the chat room. He typed:

BryNYshark: Depends on what region you're in! Spring here, about 67 degrees. Where are you?
YEMI402: Are you really an American?
BryNYshark: Yes.
YEMI402: Wow! I am smiling in my heart. This machine is amazing to me and I can't believe that I can talk to people around the world. Where I come from this is very new.
BryNYshark: Where's that?
YEMI402: Far, far away in a place called Kirkos. It is in Ethiopia.
BryNYshark: You're on the other side of the globe. What's your name?
YEMI402: At birth they named me Yemiate. Everyone calls me Yemi.
BryNYshark: Cool. I'm Brian.
YEMI402: Where in America are you, Brian?
BryNYshark: New York.

Brian noticed the third visitor in the chat room logged off, and waited for the return reply.

YEMI402: Wow! I have learned of that place. It must be exciting to live in America.

BryNYshark: It's cool.

YEMI402: I want to visit there one day. I am just learning how this system of the Internet works. It was fortunate for me that I was selected.

BryNYshark: You had to be selected to use the computer?

YEMI402: Yes and there is only room for a few.

BryNYshark: You must be a smart dude.

YEMI402: I am laughing to you. It is because I can read and write that I have been selected to learn the computer by Christian Missionaries that have come to my village.

BryNYshark: Word?

YEMI402: Yes I can read words.

BryNYshark: I know, but I meant something else. Okay, forget it.

YEMI402: What does 'word' mean when used in singular? I am trying to become familiar with the rules of grammar.

BryNYshark: It's a slang term we use. It's like saying, "really" or "I can't believe it!" Or, "are you serious?"

YEMI402: I think I understand. What is your nationality?

BryNYshark: I'm like you, only I am American.

YEMI402: Now I am really glad. You are an African in America.

BryNYshark: That's me.

YEMI402: What is your age?

BryNYshark: Sixteen. How old are you?

YEMI402: I am smiling again. We are close to the same. I am around sixteen to eighteen years of age.

BryNYshark: You don't know?

YEMI402: No, not for sure. Because of the war the public records in my village were destroyed.

BryNYshark: What about your family? Don't they know?

YEMI402: I do not have a family. My mother and father died when I was a small boy. All of my friends here are without parents.

Brian thought for a moment, wondering how to respond.

BryNYshark: Sorry to hear that.

YEMI402: I am sorry too but there are so many of us we have become an orphanage village. I cannot wait to tell my friends that I can talk to someone in America.

BryNYshark: It's an experience for me, too.

YEMI402: Tomorrow we will learn how to write a letter on the computer and mail it to someone else.

BryNYshark: That's called email.

YEMI402: Email is short for electronic mail?

BryNYshark: That's right.

YEMI402: Can I send the letter I write to you?

BryNYshark: Sure.

YEMI402: Our teacher will instruct us on how to send it on a separate document.

BryNYshark: That's called attaching a document to your email.

YEMI402: You seem to know very much about computers.

BryNYshark: I guess you can say that.

YEMI402: Maybe you can teach me some things.

BryNYshark: No problem. Let me know what you need.

YEMI402: I want to know more about America.

BryNYshark: I can help you with that.

YEMI402: This is good. I'm so excited.

BryNYshark: You got a lot of energy for this time of night, Yemi.

YEMI402: It is morning, bright and sunny here.

BryNYshark: It's after midnight here. Almost 2am.

YEMI402: You are up late. Why?

BryNYshark: Just got some things on my mind, feel me?

YEMI402: How is it possible to feel you?

BryNYshark: Sorry. That's another slang term we use. It means do you understand me, feel what I feel?

YEMI402: Okay, I understand. It's like when I learned the news that the missionaries had chosen me to learn about computers. It was on my mind all night and I did not sleep.

BryNYshark: That's it.

YEMI402: I will return to the chat room tomorrow to speak with you.

BryNYshark: Not sure if I will be online at that time.

YEMI402: I will then try the next day.

Brian thought for a moment. He typed:

BryNYshark: You will need my email address to communicate with me like that. You can't send it to me on the chat line. Your teacher will explain that to you. You can send me a message through email, but we cannot talk interactively like we are doing now. It will be like, you write me and I write you back. Get it?

YEMI402: I get it, yes.

BryNYshark: Write this email address down.

YEMI402: I got it.

BryNYshark: Be strong. Later.

YEMI402: I will say good-bye for now.

"GET UP!" ordered Mr. Parker, bolting into Brian's room at 6:40am, startling him out of his sleep. Donned with a navy blue pinstripe suit and a bright white shirt, he was ready for work. "Here's the itinerary."

"Huh?" Brian grunted, groggy and disoriented.

"The bank's opening a new branch in about five weeks. We're expecting about three or four hundred people . . . and that's gonna mean at least a hundred kids. We'll rent the outfit and you'll be the clown."

Mr. Parker's strong cologne revived him to full cognition. "What are you talking about, Dad?"

"The grand opening's in Harlem. There's going to be food, games and all that. So while the adults are opening up accounts and taking care of business, we're gonna need some entertainment to keep the kids busy. I was going to hire a clown but then I thought about it." Mr. Parker paused and added something to his list. "I can have you do it . . . from nine to three."

"I don't want to be a clown, Dad."

Mr. Parker looked him dead in the eye. "That's what you do every day. Play games, fool around; you don't follow rules . . . so here's a chance to do publicly what you do best."

Brian sighed, removed the covers and placed his feet on the floor. "Am I getting paid for this?"

"Paid?" his father asked, turning sharply. "You already got paid . . . with my money that you spent on those video games that I told you *not* to buy. Now you're going to earn it. Here," he said, handing Brian the itinerary. "Hold on to that."

"THINK YOU can get away from me?" Brian challenged, hurling at the new assassins. At 4:49pm Champion GameSpot was charged with zealous gamers. Brian shot viciously, talking to himself. "I got something for you . . . uh oh! Here I come." Feeling superhuman with one of the best arcade joysticks he shot three bullets striking one target. "C'mon, c'mon, c'mon," Brian jabbered, his voice drowning in the sea of noise. "I'ma get both of y'all!"

"You winnin'?" Ricky said, appearing out of nowhere.

"What took you so long?" Brian asked. "I told you to meet me at four thirty."

"My moms wanted me to pick up some tiles for her."

"Gotchu workin'?"

"Yeah, I had to carry these—"

"Hold up," Brian said, gracefully annihilating the competition. "There you go. And this is what I got for your partner," he said, striking without mercy.

"To the left!" Ricky warned as a bullet felled his man to the ground. "You hit!"

"You jinxed me!" Brian fired out, pounding the side of the machine.

"No I didn't."

"Yes you did!"

"I did not," Ricky argued, handing Brian a white paper bag.

"What's this?"

"Sweet rolls."

"From Mama Sita?" Brian asked, calming his tone.

"Yeah."

"I already told you. I'd marry your mother if Santiago wasn't in the way," he said digging in the bag.

"You'd have three other men to get through first," Ricky chuckled.

Brian was easy to forgive, especially when his best friends' mother offered him food. Not only was she one of the best cooks he'd ever known, her decadent desserts were to die for. The first bite of the soft sweet roll warmed his insides. "I would be three hundred pounds if my moms worked in a bakery," Brian mumbled, eyeing other games as they were making their way outside.

"You gettin' close," Manuel teased.

"You a funny man now, huh?"

Unexpectedly, Brian caught a glimpse of Jeremy Winters and redirected his course.

"I've been looking for you, yo."

"Why?" asked the fair skinned African American that everyone thought was Spanish. Jeremy was obsessed by the in-car view as he raced the vehicle in excess of 118 miles.

"What's that dude's name you introduced me to . . . asking all the questions about streaming?" Brian was fishing.

"Description?"

"The white dude . . . the one who was picking my brain."

"Key word, white," said Jeremy. "Talkin' about T-Man?"

"Yeah, that's what they call him. Detectives came to my house asking me all these questions about him and I didn't make the connection—"

"Detectives?" he asked, taking off his shades. Indoors or outdoors, he always wore them.

"Yo, he's got some young girl doin' porn online and hittin' me back and forth, trying to learn how to do it. Now they're trackin' him and all his contacts looking for the players."

"T-Man's always into somethin'," Jeremy said.

"If you was up on it, why didn't you let me know?"

"Negative. He don't talk to me like that."

"Okay, so he might be keepin' it low. But when you rollin' like that you need to guard your moves, know what I'm sayin'?"

"True."

"That's fowl," mumbled Ricky.

"I'ma give him the benefit," Brian said. "Probably thought he was undercover. I tell people all the time, anything you do on the net leaves a trail."

"I haven't seen him," said Jeremy, putting his glasses back on.

"Nobody has. He's got to go to court now."

"Word?"

"It's what they told me."

"That's right, dude is eighteen," Jeremy recalled.

"You know what that means," Ricky chuckled.

Brian had taken his last bite and crushed the bag with one hand before tossing it in the garbage. "Mess around and he'll be taking a real long vacation."

"Let's get outta here," Ricky said.

"Tell him I'm looking for him when you see him," Brian said, walking away.

"Dude is weird," Ricky remarked.

"A little strange sometimes . . . but he's cool."

Outside, there was a crowd gathering.

"That's Razi!" A young man they called Aaron shouted.

"Ah man, it is," Brian acknowledged brightly. "Razi's home."

Everyone swarmed to the young man from Telham Park who had been drafted to the NBA more than two years ago. He wasn't a starter but received several opportunities to prove himself during the season.

"Look how big he is now," Ricky said as they hustled to get closer to him.

"What's he doing here?" One of the older girls asked who frequented the game room with her younger sister.

"His uncle's in the hospital," somebody replied.

"You talkin' about Uncle Percy?" Brian turned and asked. "Yeah."

Brian's father moonlighted as a special armed agent for business and political VIP's at Uncle Percy's security agency when he first retired from the military some years ago.

"Good thing I got here late," Ricky said. "We would have missed him."

"Twenty-nine!" Brian greeted, stealing an opportunity to embrace him. "Whas poppin'?"

"Brian! Hi you, man. How's your family?" His ivory complexion had turned copper, like he'd been basting in a tropical sun.

"Everybody's good, good. Happy to see you, man."

"Dimples!" one of the girls yelled out from the back of the crowd.

The six foot seven maverick was clean cut and bulky in his designer T-shirt, jeans, and white sneakers. Those same muscular arms he used to shoot three pointers were solid like guns.

"When you gonna dunk fifty on Detroit?" a young man attending a military school in Long Island asked, coming between them. "I had some money on that game."

"Whassup Soldier Boy!"

Wearing an expensive watch and diamond studs, Razi reeked of money and success. Soon, he had become buried in a crowd of spectators.

Brian inhaled a whiff of the cinnamon fragrance that had seeped out of the elegantly crafted and gleaming Escalade parked out front. "That joint is fire, yo!"

"Must be his bodyguard," Ricky surmised, acknowledging the big, dark figure talking on his cell phone beside the silky black SUV. "Can you believe that?"

"Unbelievable," Brian chuckled. "Razi, with his own personal muscle. That's big."

"See his girl?" Ricky asked, mesmerized by the stunning beauty they glimpsed at through the open window. "That's drop dead right there!"

"When you sign a multi-million dollar contract you get top of the line ev'ra thing," said Brian.

"That's real," Ricky agreed. "I would trade places with him any day."

"That's a good look," Brian said, thinking of the mysterious girl he was longing to meet. "I'm proud of him. So what did you find out for me?"

"Oh yeah," he remembered, pulling out a list. "You got three churches in that area. There's a Catholic Church, St. Ambrose, a Presbyterian one—"

"Could be any one of them," Brian said. "How do I know?"

"No, but this is what I figured out, look at this map. That's about eight blocks from the ninth street train station. The other two are further away."

"Okay."

"And now you owe me money 'cause I called them up. They told me they have a breakfast program from Monday to Friday. But they only do dinner on Saturdays. That's probably what you saw."

"Think she works there?"

"She's doin' something there."

"Good lookin' . . . iight. Gotta go. I'ma catch that same train when I go back up there. If she doesn't get on, I'm going back to that church. I'll stand on that line if I have to."

"Do what you gotta do."

"Yeah . . ." Brian said thinking. "That food looked pretty good, too."

"And we know you don't ever turn down a meal."

"Iight, man."

They shook hands and parted.

LATE THAT NIGHT, Brain was still up thinking and munching on snacks while browsing through a computer game magazine. When he was sure that his parents had fallen asleep, he slipped down to the basement and signed on and found Yemi online.

YEMI402: Hello my friend. I know that you are up late in the night in New York because I discovered that our time difference is seven hours ahead of yours.

BryNYshark: That's good. You taught me something I didn't know. What time is it there now?

YEMI402: It is 8:18am and I have finished all of my assignments. We begin our day at early dawn while it is still cool. Did you receive the document I sent to you?

BryNYshark: Yes. In my reply I sent you the names of some web sites to check out. Look in your mailbox.

YEMI402: Thank you. I will locate it after we eat our afternoon meal.

BryNYshark: What's for lunch?

YEMI402: We will eat injera.

BryNYshark: What kind of food is that?

YEMI402: It is what we call sourdough flatbread. Ethiopian's love it.

BryNYshark: Sounds good.

YEMI402: It is. We are excited because we will have vegetable stew with it and that does not occur often.

BryNYshark: What do you usually eat?

YEMI402: Whatever we can find.

BryNYshark: What do you get filled up on?

YEMI402: There is no such practice. We have to ration food because we do not know when more is coming.

BryNYshark: What happens if no food comes?

YEMI402: We don't eat.

BryNYshark: How do you make it . . . being hungry?

YEMI402: You adapt. It is not so bad . . . if it doesn't go on too long.

BryNYshark: Why is there so much hunger in your country?

YEMI402: The problem is the cyclical drought. When there is no rain or it comes late the harvest are not good and most people here live off the land. And then the coffee crop is yielding very little return in dollars now from the export.

BryNYshark: Why not?

YEMI402: I do not know. It has been rumored about greedy western hands. And the people are not educated to adequately trade so it is easy to be taken advantage of.

BryNYshark: Does the government help you?

YEMI402: That is another problem. Ethiopia receives tons of food every year, so they say. But it's not being spread around where it is needed most, especially in remote villages like the one I live in.

BryNYshark: That's tough.

YEMI402: Yes. The days can be long, especially when the hunger turns to starvation. Without energy you feel too heavy for your legs to carry you. That's when you get desperate and you might eat grass or wild weeds or even sometimes pods.

BryNYshark: Money can buy you everything you need over here. Let me send you some cash to get something to eat.

YEMI402: If it were only that simple. To receive any communication like letters or packages, it is a three hour trail each way. And there is no guarantee that the money would land in my hands and even if it did, we have no where to spend it. When there is a drought, even the food markets are bare.

BryNYshark: Wish I could help you.

YEMI402: Thank you, but we need to find ways to feed ourselves. This is why I dream of education so that I can learn the way.

BryNYshark: How can you concentrate when you're hungry?

YEMI402: You condition your mind as best you can and it is never easy. It is my hope that I may one day be able to migrate to America and a school will accept me. Then I could learn agriculture and find ways to drive the economy. And then I can give my people the right education to decrease the HIV/AIDS epidemic.

BryNYshark: Without food or medicine how do y'all survive?

YEMI402: Many of us don't. You could be talking to a dead man.

BryNYshark: Yo, don't talk like that. You're spooking me.

YEMI402: This is our reality, my friend. We live for the day. When we receive food, especially chicken, it is a festival. We are smiling and very happy. Then, tomorrow, we will have to think about food.

BryNYshark: I hope there are no worries about food tomorrow.

YEMI402: As long as the missionaries are here, we expect there will be a meal each day. It is time to go. So long for now, my friend.

BryNYshark: Peace.

four

"**Y**a heard about that dude that got his laptop stolen?" Brian asked his friends, sliding into his seat with a tray filled with nachos and a colossal burger at the Battlerock Café. "It was all over the news."

Chang, Malyck and Rekcah were already eating.

"No, what happened?" asked Malyck.

"Yo, he put his laptop down to buy some magazine, right? Looked away for a split second to pay for it and somebody snatched it."

"Bad move," said Chang. "That's why I keep mine chained to my belt."

"Lucky for him, yo, he was a tech. Logged into that joint everyday by remote and watched, waiting for some kind of clue to identify him. This idiot's touring all these sites, playing games and checking out porn. Three days later he registers for some free seminar, keyed all his information in and led the cops right to his front door."

"Imagine the look on that dude when he opened the door," said Rekcah. "Good afternoon officers, how can I help you?"

On the television, a tennis match captured the other patrons' attention while Malyck captured theirs explaining how he had earned so much money online collecting change.

"You got a dime, quarter, no donation is too small," he told them while Rekcah filmed the exchange on his videocam, "and these donations will help finance small businesses in third world countries. Twenty five or thirty dollars is all some families need to get a start."

Malyck was an inspiration to the group. Despite the Parkinson's, he remained focused in his efforts to help the less fortunate. And girls flocked to him like honey to bees. He was humble, and insisted that girls were drawn to his dedication and hard work and it had nothing to do with his amazingly handsome looks. They always parted feeling motivated to think about ways to use technology to help humanity.

AT 4:22pm, the train pulled into West 10th Street where Brian hoped to see the beautiful girl. He had meandered through clusters of commuters getting on and off the train at all the stops but there was no sign of her. Stalled at the station for several minutes, the female conductor announced the plan for the local train to switch to the express track. Discouraged and indecisive, Brian watched hordes of people spill out of the train across the platform when suddenly, the gorgeous face of the ravishing dazzler rushed by.

He moved quickly in the hopes of getting close enough to stir up a conversation before she exited the turnstile. But the hordes of commuters denied him access to her.

Out in the street Brian trailed close behind, admiring her swaggering walk.

"Wait a second," he heard her say, stopping suddenly. She switched her cell phone from the left ear to the right and sighed frustrated. "I can't hear you, say that again . . . hello . . . hello—"

"Your battery's dying. You can use my phone," Brian offered, seizing the moment.

She glanced over at him, appearing more stunning up close. "Ah, that's okay," she said, a pleasant but cautious smile that appeared and disappeared in an instant. "I'll be able to charge it in a minute . . . but thanks anyway."

"I've seen you before," Brian said. "I think it was about three weeks ago."

"Really?" She frowned curiously, her disbelief obvious. "You don't look familiar," she said and then continued walking.

"No, it was you . . . when the train was delayed," he replied following her. "There was a fire."

". . .Yeah, I do remember that," she recalled, easing into a smile. "That was kinda scary."

"It was for a minute. You live around here?"

"No. How about you?" she asked.

"Nah, I come up here to go to the Apple Store sometimes," Brian replied, which was partially true. He and his friends from the camp had visited the store once.

"That's where I go to take film workshops."

"You make movies?"

"Not exactly. My camera is my hobby. Like I'm working on this video right now."

"What are you shooting?" Brian asked, walking evenly with her stride.

"My father's turning fifty this year so I'm doing like a mini bio of his life."

"Oh that's a family heirloom right there."

"Guess you could call it that."

"Where you headed to now?" He felt so comfortable talking to her; the questions just fell out of his mouth.

"Work."

"Can I go with you?"

She smiled showing her beautiful teeth, curtained by glossy, sensual lips. "Actually . . . yeah. We could use some extra hands."

"I'm just kiddin'."

"No, really, we could use the help."

"Where do you work?"

"United Front Episcopal."

"That sounds like a church?"

"Uh huh, I volunteer there . . . serving meals to homeless people."

"That's what you were doing there," Brian realized and stopped cold. And when she laid her soft, glistening eyes on him, like kryptonite to Superman, he was weakened.

"What was I doing where?" she asked.

"That's not what I meant," Brian quickly retracted. "I was just trying to make the connection in my mind to a church . . . food and the homeless—forget it."

"Okay. Anyway, we serve the community," she continued. "If they're hungry, we feed them."

"How many hours do you put in?"

"The meals are served everyday, but I only do the Saturday dinner shift. When you finish at the store, you're more than welcome to come and help."

"What store?" he asked, suffering a temporary memory lapse.

"The Apple Store . . . where you're going."

"What am I thinking?" Brian snapped, transferring his gaze from the Asian man with the violin. He was playing a romantic instrumental with a hint of gypsy jazz. "Maybe I can help out for a few."

"I'll give you the address," she said and stopped. "So when you're finished you can—"

"It might be better for me to do it now and go to the store later."

"You sure?"

"Yeah, I'm supposed to meet somebody later on," he sidelined, camouflaging the reality of his curfew.

"Where do you live?"

"Brooklyn. Telham Park."

"I know where you are. I've been there before."

"What about you?"

"I live uptown . . . off 5th Avenue, by Central Park."

"I should have guessed it. Only people who live in the city say uptown and downtown. We just say Manhattan."

Until now, Brian had never met anyone of color living on the Upper East Side. His father will probably flip about his lateness, he thought, but any punishment was worth the opportunity to spend time with the young lady whose name he didn't know.

"I'm Brian."

"Monet."

"You look like a Monet."

"What does that look like?"

"Pretty."

Monet turned away blushing and then shot Brian a quick shy glance. "You know how to make a girl smile."

"Like you don't hear that all the time, c'mon."

"Not really," she replied, tossing her head both ways as they crossed the street.

Brian couldn't take his eyes off of her lovely face. Her friendly manner felt familiar, as if he'd known her before.

"I have two quick stops to make before we get there, okay?"

"Cool," Brian agreed.

"Picking up donations from the church, if you're wondering."

"Huh?"

"That's what I do each week. I go to the neighborhood stores and collect donations for the church."

"Oh that's cool."

"Still wanna come?"

"Let's do it."

"I WON'T tell if you don't," the crooked faced, dirty red, elderly man said, handing Brian his plate for a second helping.

Brian nodded affirmatively wearing a plastic cap on his head, an apron wrapped around his front and plastic gloves on his hands. He was an official volunteer now and kindly served him a generous portion of meatloaf.

"Can . . . can you give me just a little bit more of that gravy, please?" His frail body leaned to one side as if he had had a stroke.

"I think I can do that," Brian obliged, dipping the silver ladle.

"Mmm that's nice," the gentleman remarked, watching the gravy roll smoothly over the meat.

They both knew that second helpings were not allowed until everyone had been fed.

Homeless people didn't seem to talk much, Brian noticed. In fact, it seemed almost quiet in the stark basement. Poverty wasn't so obvious with some of them, but looking closer, subtle signs of hardship became apparent. Especially on the children's smudged clothes, beat up shoes, and the offensive odors carried by a few.

Life is totally unpredictable, Brian thought. One minute he's feasting on his favorite junk food in the heart of Times Square with computer geeks, and the next minute he's serving food in a church basement to homeless people.

"I see you're catching on," Monet whispered from behind.

"What's that?"

"We always let Mr. Hardigan have seconds."

Brian felt good working, helping others in need, particularly with a beautiful partner like Monet. He stole glances of her serving and socializing as if it had been her calling.

After serving more than a hundred people the afternoon sun had dropped into evening. Two hours had gone by just like that. Once the people filed out, leaving the volunteers to the clean up effort, Brian discovered a diverse group of people from all walks of life. And true to his character, he conversed easily, leaving them feeling as if they had found a new friend.

ON THEIR way home, people leisurely strolled the streets in the twilight. The cool breeze of summer air belonged to lovers on their way to eating, music and dancing.

"You can still make the store," Monet said. "They're usually open until about eight, I think."

"Another time," said Brian. "I'm supposed to meet somebody later."

"I hope I didn't take you away from what you had to do or—"

"Nah, it's cool."

"Your first time volunteering?"

"Yep."

"Hard to believe people rely on soup kitchens to eat."

". . . Unbelievable."

"Gives you a different outlook on things, right?"

"To be honest I . . . I never really . . . processed in my mind like what it would be like to be hungry. Ay, did you see that woman in the wheelchair?" Brian asked, thinking of the helpless white woman who had one arm, no use of her legs, and was overweight.

"You're talking about Esther. She wheels herself here every Saturday for a hot meal. Can you imagine?"

"Probably likes the company, too."

"Exactly."

Monet felt secure in the Brian's presence, a kindred spirit of sorts. After all, how many strangers would have given up their time on the spur of the moment to help feed the homeless? "Appreciate your help."

"It's all good. Ay let me ask you somethin'. What made you start doing this?"

"I don't know," she replied. "Something I always wanted to do, I guess. People have helped us out in the past . . . and it made all the difference in the world."

"You mean like . . . helped your family?"

"Well, yeah . . . our people, too. Sometimes you just need that extra hand to get you to the next step, especially when you're really trying and the odds are against you."

"That's real," said Brian as they descended into the subway station. "And you're seriously dedicated to it."

"Have to be."

There was nothing false or pretentious about her. She was a genuinely selfless human being who didn't think twice about sacrificing her time.

"Go ahead," Brian said, swiping his metro card and allowing her to move through the turnstile at his expense.

"Thanks."

"I gave you my email address, right?" Brian asked as they slowed to a stop.

"Got it." she replied, pressing her gaze on him.

I'm not ready to part from you yet. Look at you . . . your mesmerizing eyes, those sweet lips. I want to take you—"

"And thanks again . . . for everything," she said feeling the urge to embrace him, but decided to hold back. She was glad to have met a young man whose interests extended beyond her physical appearance . . . so she thought.

Brian was entranced by her inner and outer beauty. "So hit me up," he said as they parted.

"I will. Definitely. Coming next week?" she asked and stopped again. People were rushing in between them.

"I might," Brian shouted.

"Okay, later."

"Iight."

Monet flounced out of his view down the northbound stairs leaving Brian to a whirlwind of thoughts as if he'd been dreaming.

IT WAS after eight when Brian arrived home. He quietly opened the door and was unexpectedly met by his father coming up the stairs from the basement wearing his sweats and perspiring from a workout.

"Where were you?" He asked, glancing over at the wall clock. His muscles were swollen, making him appear heavier.

"I was helping somebody out."

"You forgot about our deal?" Mr. Parker asked, inching toward him with that glower in his eyes that could sometimes make Brian tremble.

"No, but I didn't think I had to—"

"I was being lenient letting you go to lunch," he said, removing his weightlifting straps.

"And I came home."

"You were supposed to come straight home. Look at the time," he said, wiping his slippery face.

"I was doin' a friend a favor."

"Helping the dude with the porn again?"

"No Dad. How many times I have to tell you—"

"What!" Mr. Parker scowled.

"I'm sayin' Dad, I didn't have anything to do with that. You keep drillin' me."

"You're still wrong . . . and if you couldn't get here in time, you could've called."

"You took my phone," Brian reminded him, even though he had smuggled it out of his parents' bedroom and it was still on. *Please do not ring phone or I'm finished!*

"Public phones still exist."

"It's hard to find one, but you're right, I wasn't thinking to look—"

"That's the problem," lamented Mr. Parks, wiping his neck and arms. "You're never thinking when it comes down to doing what you're supposed to do. It's no different than—"

Get real, Dad! So what I didn't come home on time. Don't you know I just met a girl that's got my heart doing summersaults? Somebody I would walk ten miles for, serve meals to strangers with and give up everything I've got. I'm walking on the edge and this is all you have to talk about.

"I gotta go to the bathroom," Brian said, and charged up the stairs. He turned off the phone, placed it back in his parents' bedroom closet, and retreated to his room. There he emptied his knapsack and bit into the burger he doggy bagged as he thought about Monet.

"You just added another week," his father told him entering the room. Mr. Parker had a thing about privacy in his house. He believed he had open access to every crack and crevice in his house, particularly Brian's room.

"C'mon Dad," Brian pleaded. "Your gonna hold that—"

"Rules are the rules and you gotta learn."

"How 'bout if I clean out the yard?"

"What are we . . . making deals here?" Mr. Parker was not amused, his face frowning in disbelief at Brian's irreverence. "No, you're gonna clean the yard anyway and *still* get another week."

Brian sighed and bagged his burger. "This is crazy."

"What was that?" Mr. Parker asked, halting his exit.

"Nothing, Dad. I didn't say anything."

AT 12:39am, lying across his bed, Brian was wide awake, recapping the day's events and the time spent at the church with Monet. When he was certain his parents were snoozing comfortably, he crept down in the basement to get on the Internet. There was a message awaiting him.

From: "Monet Kellman"
To: "Brian Parker"
Subject: Volunteer Work

It was nice to meet you. And lucky for United Front Episcopal, we found another trooper. Thanks for all your help . . . and the ride, too. Hope to see you next Saturday.

Oh, one more thing. **Artists of the East** are doing a fundraising event at my school in two weeks. I'll send you an evite, just in case you're interested.

Brian immediately responded.

From: "Brian Parker"
To: "Monet Kellman"
Subject: Volunteer Work

It was a good experience. Glad I could help. Saturday's not working for me. I've got some things to do. Maybe the Saturday after. Send me the evite for Thursday.

five

"Yeah!" shouted Mr. Parker smacking high-fives with four of his friends when the NBA playoff game was called into overtime. Festive Mondays were rare in the Parker household and Brian was happy to be in the company of men watching his favorite sport. It was almost midnight when the game finally ended—in a double-overtime victory—and amid the charged atmosphere, Brian volunteered to clean up. Only the real objective was to steal an opportunity to get online and connect with Yemi.

YEMI402: Hello my friend, how are you?
BryNYshark: What's up?
YEMI402: Good news has come from the missionaries today. Some organization has expressed interest in building a school in my village. This is unbelievable! Matthew tells us not to get too

excited. He says things sometimes do not work out as planned. I understand Matthew, but it feels good.

BryNYshark: I'm happy for you.

YEMI402: Thank you. I cannot imagine a real school with books and tablets and a room with a toilet. That is the kind of school that you have, right?"

BryNYshark: Yes.

YEMI402: My people have not seen new books in over twenty years. I cannot wait to get out of the hut.

BryNYShark: What's the hut?

YEMI402: That is where we learn. We work there to avoid the extreme heat, but it is sometimes very difficult. There is not much room, so very few children can attend at once. And there is talk of a well coming. This would be so wonderful.

BryNYShark: How do you get water now?

YEMI402: Mornings I fetch water in a clay pot, but up until the new well was built, it took three hours for the trip walking. When I was lucky enough to catch a ride, it was a long and rough drive over dusty roads. Now it only takes a little over an hour.

Brian was stifled by Yemi's harsh conditions and for lack of not knowing what else to say, he replied:

BryNYshark: Hopefully that's all gonna change soon.

YEMI402: Yes, I can not wait. Tell me, are you excited at the start of the day when you go to school?

BryNYshark: It's a requirement here for us so it's just an everyday thing.

YEMI402: Help me to understand how getting an education becomes an everyday thing? It is so broad, an eternity of possibilities.

BryNYshark: Dudes here don't see it like that. Too much work for them. Rather have fun.

YEMI402: What could be more fun than learning?

BryNYshark: Girls, hanging out, playing video games.

YEMI402: We like the same, except we do not have video games, but we would trade it to have education first. That is what we need to insure our future and make our conditions better.

BryNYshark: You're a smart dude.

YEMI402: Smart? Why do you call me this?

BryNYshark: The things you say make me think.

YEMI402: I speak by the things I have lived.

BryNYshark: Brothers see things totally different here.

YEMI402: It is maybe because you have many choices.

BryNYshark: Funny, because with all they have here, they're never satisfied. Always want more.

YEMI402: This is true when you have many things. The search is unending for more things. Until you find you, it is a futile effort.

BryNYshark: That heavy.

YEMI402: Yes, it weighs a lot. We have no choices here, we only hope for things to get better. When they build a school in my village we will not have to travel so far.

BryNYshark: How far is your school?

YEMI402: Two, maybe three kilometers. It takes about two hours to walk.

BryNYshark: Each way?

YEMI402: Yes.

BryNYshark: Is that why Ethiopians win all the long distance marathons over here?

YEMI402: I am smiling. You are aware of this?

BryNYshark: Yes, and so is the rest of the world. They win all the time but I thought they were just naturally gifted.

YEMI402: Part of what you say may be true. But we also have the best training ground. We pound the dirt roads and walk for miles every day to find work, food, and water and to go to school. I have to move on to our lesson now. Matthew will teach us how to do research for information today.

BryNYshark: Okay, good. Later dude.

YEMI402: Later, my friend.

LEXINGTON CONNORS Preparatory School was a three-story, brick frame building had been a factory-to-school conversion, from a historic manufacturing warehouse that had gone bankrupt. Ultra modern in its renovations, it was spacious with tall ceilings, wooden floors with a high buff, cove lighting, and bright pastel walls.

Monet and Brian walked the halls of Academe—which was more like a social club than an expensive private school—and took the elevator one level down. Female and male ushers in burgundy jackets, navy plaid skirts and navy khakis greeted them in front of a captivating promotional showcase. Colorful clusters of fantasy and horror, history, caricature, satire, nature, comic book art and photo exhibits were displayed under soft lights.

Visitors and students converged into cliques of camera shooting observers and critics taking notes. "They're gonna do a silent auction later on," Monet told Brian. "He's from

Channel Twelve," she added, pointing her eyes to the tall, white, and upright gentleman.

"This is gonna be on TV?" Brian asked.

"In the newspaper, too," Monet replied. "Meet the public relations director," she said, looking at a curly headed, medium-built white man who had just popped a salmon hors d'oeuvre in his mouth. "He's the event coordinator . . . our communications teacher too." Monet leaned into Brian and whispered. "His father's the president of RBS."

"The television station?"

"That's right."

"Ay, look at this," Brian said, enamored by the striking exhibit someone had done of the human body in neon colorful schemes.

"That's what you look like underneath your skin," Monet responded knowingly. "Let me get you something to drink."

"No thanks, I'm good," he said and was struck by the elongated faces of an exhibit entitled *The Tormented Jury*. "Ay, this group right here looks like just sentenced somebody to death."

"These are my pictures," Monet said, pulling him away. Grouped in a square of four was a set of silver framed black and white photographs of footwear. "I call it the 'Walk a Mile in My Shoes' series."

"Okay," Brian said, studying each of them thoughtfully, pondering the motive behind the concept. The photograph captured rows and rows of women shoes, various styles, sizes and colors.

"I took this shot from the balcony," she said.

"Where was this?"

"At the church, don't you recognize it?"

"Wait a minute," Brian said, perusing the background. "That's the wall next to the staircase . . . where the rest rooms are."

"Eggs-actly!"

"It's got to be forty pairs of shoes here."

"More than that. We were doing a clothes drive earlier this year and I had the job of pricing the shoes. So I separated the men's shoes from the women's and it was a funny thing."

"What . . . you discovered women's feet are larger than men's?"

Both of them smothered their laughter.

"You'd be surprised at some of the sizes of the girls' feet I know, but as I'm removing them from boxes or bags, I get a different feeling from every pair of them. Like they were all telling me a story."

"Talking shoes, huh?"

"No, you're not getting it. Like the little lace ups over here," she pointed. "You can tell they've got some miles on them. And look at these," she said inching closer to the photograph. "Someone wore the sole out of them. Get it, soul."

"I gotchu," he chuckled.

"You gotta wonder are the people who wore these shoes even alive. Too bad the shoes can't talk."

"Yeah, imagine the stories they could tell," Brian said. "How many countries they've traveled and—"

"I remember a story my father told me about his Italian friend who owns a pizza franchise. He said his father came to this country with no shoes and a dime in his pocket."

"Streets must have been real clean then."

"Sixty something years ago, I'm sure. So he gets off the boat and this man drives past him and sees him walking barefoot and stops. He takes off his shoes and gave it to him and he wore those same shoes for two years. What a story those shoes must have to tell."

"Oh, I feel you," Brian agreed.

"But check out the pink stilettos. They've got that vintage look, like they may have appeared in a Broadway performance or something . . . And look at these. They were donations from Muduri."

"Word?"

Muduri was one of the most elite shoe designers that no one could afford and any respectable *fashionista's* must have.

"Yeah, they're new."

"Look at this one," Monet directed. The shot depicted a varicolored strapped and pointed toe pump.

"Now she's got some class," Brian said.

"You could tell, right?"

"Okay, I think I see what you're sayin' about a shoe telling a story."

"You got it."

"Like this woman's confident. Kinda young . . . probably beautiful."

"I had a pair something like that," a girl said, approaching them. She was with another girl, both of whom were classmates of Monet.

"Imori!" The long legged dazzler who bared the look of a stock photo model embraced Monet lovingly. She was a talented artist that had produced a unique line of handcrafted jewelry being displayed in the smaller room behind them. Around her neck was a glass-beaded necklace with matching earrings. "That is so pretty," Monet praised, and then introduced Brian to them.

"These pictures look awesomely professional," The other girl named Montana exclaimed as she air kissed Monet. She was a blue-eyed cutie leading the *Abstinence for Teens* campaign. "Any of these shoes belong to you?"

"I don't know . . . maybe." Monet replied. "Can you match any of these styles to my optimistic, out-going personality?"

Montana inched closer, carefully observing the photographs. "Nope, it's none of these. This pair belongs to a little girl I can see. Woman, woman, older woman," she mumbled.

"A hooker," Imori interjected, pointing to the black patent leather ankle boots with the spiked silver heel.

"These are all men," Montana said pondering the third one. "This could be yours," she decided, pointing to the single shoe.

Monet laughed as Brian suddenly realized he had accurately profiled Monet by looking at her shoe.

"C'mon let me take a picture," Imori suggested.

Moving in closely together they posed and smiled.

"This'll be worth a lot of money one day," Imori said, framing the shot. "Everybody say billions."

"Billions!"

"A BUNCH of us are going to Christina's, wanna come?" asked a girl named Skylar, seated next to Monet at the auction.

"I don't know. I'll have to see what my friend wants to do.

Brian was busy doing the math. Some of the adults paid prohibitive amounts of money for student's artwork, which in actuality was their contribution to the student's journey to Asia, the objective of the fundraising event. One woman, the eccentric kind who was into animal art, paid over a thousand dollars for a simple photograph of an elephant that had been taken in Africa by one of the students during a summer Safari. Monet was shocked and thrilled that someone's interest in shoes would ring to the tune of five hundred dollars. That's how much someone paid for her collection.

"I like the way y'all do things around here," Brian whispered. "You at thirty thousand already."

"That's nothing," she said. "We're not finished. Hey, wanna go to a party after this?"

"Where?"

"One of my friends' house."

Brian was already doubtful that he'd make it home by curfew, but an 'after party'? In the midst of great company and a new experience, the desire to be with the fascinating and gorgeous stranger stood ahead of his better judgment. "I'm with it," he decided.

PLANS FOR attending a party at Christina's Upper East Side brownstone unexpectedly changed when they found out a group of boring geeks would be there. They hopped in a cab and decided to go to Jonathan's instead.

The 25th story unit of the East River Front Towers— further downtown—was a nine hundred square foot one bedroom connected to Jonathan's parents' three-bedroom condo. Brian mulled over chips and crackers with dips, buffalo wings and nachos, lo mein and egg rolls spread over the marble counter while keeping one eye on the colorful arcade, set within the navy blue and white décor of the swank living room.

Jonathan appeared from the outdoor terrace carrying a six-pack of beer and several bottles of wine with labels that Brian was unfamiliar with. Cork screws popped and bottle tops flicked and a Thursday night party was underway.

"You've been here before?" Brian asked Monet observing her familiarity in the kitchen. She removed two glasses out of the upper right hand corner cabinet and opened the cutlery drawer and pulled out several forks.

"Oh yeah," she replied, as they planted themselves in high back swivel stools at the kitchen bar. "Jonathan doesn't need a reason to party. If he scores on a test, it's a celebration. If he bombs on the SAT prep, he throws a shindig. Says it gets him motivated to study . . . and other things too," she giggled softly.

Gazing into black laminate cabinetry, Brian wondered how the recent course of events and his new story will now read, beginning with Monet.

"Water?" she asked, pouring a bottle of the sparking thirst quencher in a glass.

"I'll have a soda," Brian replied, slowly swiveling the stool, observing the decor. "Now this is a crib."

"Yeah," Monet agreed. "Well you know his parents have money. They design these luxury yachts and travel all over the world . . . which is why he can throw all these parties."

The doorbell was a rendition of Beethoven's 5th symphony ringing loud throughout the unit. Jonathan came out of his bedroom, greeting his guests with his yorkie in his arms. Several more people entered and in no time twenty people had gathered. Thumping rap shot out of Bose speakers and the fever to move grew contagious.

"You dance?" Monet asked when the music slowed down, gently swerving her hips.

"Me, nah, but I see you do," he said, admiring her gracefulness and timely motion.

"C'mon," she said, pulling Brian to his feet and winding their way to an open area in the living room. She wrapped her arms around his neck, inviting him to hold her. "It's just me and you," she whispered.

Brian grooved in sync with her rhythm, resisting the temptation to pull her close. Her pearly eyes communicated a language of their own as they danced to the romantic ballad. "Ever been to The Vessel?" she asked.

"I heard about it but . . . I don't do clubs. My friends go but . . ."

In a circular two-step Brain caught a glimpse of the star wars challenge through the arcade window, an East river skyline, a 52-inch flat screen TV, and a street scene in Spain radiantly depicted in an oil painting.

Brian gave no thought to the time, his curfew, nor anticipated his fathers' brutal admonishments. Holding Monet, he was in a place where he wanted to stay.

BRIAN WAS wide awake at 12:47am almost feeling inhabited by Monet. The unforgettable experience, and the smell of her lingering perfume, obscured the confrontation he had with his father. She was present in his every thought: beside him she walked, in a crowd there she appeared, passing restaurants they were eating, on the train he sat beside her. The nickel he picked up off the ground was theirs to share. When Brian heard his mother retire to her room he tipped down to the basement and found Yemi on line. It was 1:13am.

YEMI402: I feel something different about you. Is everything going well?

BryNYshark: I had a fight with my father so I'm just chillin'.

YEMI402: Meaning to lower the temperature?

BryNYshark: Yeah, something like that.

YEMI402: To have a father is a privilege.

BryNYshark: Sometimes.

YEMI402: I vaguely remember my father.

BryNYshark: What happened to him?

YEMI402: It was told to me that he was kidnapped to fight in the war between Ethiopia and Eritrea. He must have been killed because he was never seen again. You are so fortunate to have a father.

BryNYshark: I guess.

YEMI402: You are not for certain?

BryNYshark: He won't let me breathe.

YEMI402: That is only to keep you contained. Imagine if he were not there?

BryNYshark: Yeah, I could live without all his rules.

YEMI402: Do you think he missed your age?

BryNYshark: What?

YEMI402: Do you think he was not young once, feeling just the same?

BryNYshark: It was different in his time.

YEMI402: There is nothing new under the sun. Your father knows better because he's been there before you. I know it well because so many of the children in my village cling to me and I almost know their thoughts. I remember my father could not make a move without me. I wanted to walk like him, talk like him, be strong like him and even have the feel of his hands. Do you feel me?

BryNYshark: Uh oh, you're catching on. Yes, I can relate.

YEMI402: Without a father you get confused in your manhood, and with no guide, who will lead you in the difficult times? We are men and with no discipline we go wild. Who can save us, except our fathers? So when he puts his foot on your chest, be grateful. That is a saying of ours.

BryNYshark: We say the same thing over here. Ay, you sound like somebody's father. That's amazing because we're the same age.

YEMI402: Maybe I've been assigned as one, to the children of the village. Hopefully one day I will be able to provide a better life for them.

BryNYshark: What's the plan?

YEMI402: I would like to organize a sports program for boys and girls. And I want to use those same teams to do work in the village.

BryNYshark: Doing what?

YEMI402: Cleaning up improper sanitation. It is the human waste that concerns us a great deal. The disease it brings costs human lives.

Brian felt squeamish in his stomach.

BryNYshark: I didn't realize that was a problem.

YEMI402: We don't have latrines here or proper sanitation like you do.

BryNYshark: So where do you—"

Brian changed his mind and deleted his question.

BryNYshark: What does it cost to build a latrine?

YEMI402: A traditional pit latrine costs $60 but there is a woman in a nearby village who has built an arborloo with a hand washing facility. The slab costs about $4. It is not the latrine alone. It is the lack of water that makes having a latrine very difficult. Sanitation for us is as important as food and water.

BryNYshark: Wish I could do more.

YEMI402: Maybe you can one day. In the meantime we rely on missionary groups and occasional government aid.

BryNYshark: You're a special dude. Something good is coming to you.

YEMI402: On those words I will return to my studies. Rest well my friend.

BryNYshark: Have a good, productive day, my man!

six

"If you're going home, jump in," shouted Ricky's older brother Orlando, offering Brian a ride. Like clockwork he was at Telham Park High School every Monday to take his younger brother to work.

"Whas good, whas good," Brian asked, crawling into the back seat of the old Toyota rumbling with Latin salsa. He offered his hand for a quick pound.

"I've been tryin' to catch up to you," Brian said to Ricky. He hadn't seen him all day.

"I was working with Rodriguez on the—"

"Check this out," Brian said, displaying the picture of him and Monet he'd taken at the gallery on his Blackberry. "What'd I tell you?" *Click.* "I told you she look good. Thought I was jokin'. Look at this one." *Click.*

"Slow down, yo. Give me a chance to look—"

Click. "And look at this, me and her together. Don't hate."

"That's where she goes to school?"

"Yeah. Ay, you gotta see how they livin'."

"Cool . . . she's nice."

"Betta than nice."

"She looks like she could be Egyptian or something."

"Didn't I tell you she was a Goddess? Listen up next time. Ya might learn somethin'."

Ricky was laughing. "You actin' like you never had a girl before."

"Not like this," Brian beamed, admiring the picture of her. "I like the way she handles herself, yo. She look betta than all the girls in Telham Park," he declared. "Even Bianca. Yo, I'ma marry this girl."

"You bringin' her out on Sunday for the show?"

"I don't know. My people got me locked in," he replied, drawn to the car that pulled up next to them at the red light, and then sped off into a right turn." Yo, that looked just like T-Man."

"The one that got you in trouble," Ricky asked.

"Yeah."

"So you're not gonna be there?" he asked, jolting Brian out of his thoughts.

"I don't know. I might get my moms to bring me out."

"At least you got your phone back."

"Nah, I snatch it out of their closet when they leave for work. Can't be without my phone."

"You live dangerous, yo," said Ricky as they pulled up to his house.

"Maybe, maybe, ayo," Brian said as he got out and slapped Orlando's hand. "Make that baby dance."

Orlando reversed the lowrider and pulled out in the middle of the street slowly. Then he raised the car and performed a single pump hop hitting some thirty inches.

"Double pump it," Brian yelled as he ran alongside of the hydraulic vehicle.

Elevated again, Orlando made the car look as if it were hopping until he reached the red light. There, he pumped the vehicle to the rhythm of his music in an icy smooth groove.

"That's sweet!" Brian marveled, roused by the sport. "I'ma try to make it on Sunday."

THE THOUGHT of getting up bright and early on a stormy Saturday morning was just that—a thought. Nestled between cotton sheets and a goose down comforter, Brian could hear the rain beating against the window and was lulled back to sleep. Lost in a dream, he and Monet were somewhere in a never-ending field of spring wildflowers playing like children, her innocent laughter bursting loudly. He gathered up a bouquet of the bright yellow Marsh Marigolds and reached for her but she ran away. Chasing her, he was lured into the glory of a botanical garden with colorful flowers and curative herbs that had the pungent smell of breakfast sausages. Suddenly awakened, he felt disappointed at the interruption and lay still, hoping to return to his romantic bliss. But the anticipation of his mother's blueberry pancakes and sausages sobered him to full cognition and he made his way downstairs.

"Mornin' Dad."

"It's almost afternoon," he replied, lying on his back underneath the kitchen sink.

Mr. Parker had a phobia about things being broken or malfunctioning in the house. It made him paranoid, like it might be an omen that things were falling apart in his life.

"Ma left already?" Brain asked, lifting the lids of containers finding blueberry pancakes, sausages, and bacon.

"Uh huh."

Brian prepared a pan to scramble the seasoned egg batter he found in the refrigerator. "Have you eaten, Dad?"

"Not yet," he grunted. "I wanna finish replacing this seal."

"Yeah, I saw water leaking underneath there yesterday."

"Then you should have fixed it. What if I weren't here?"

"I would have called somebody."

"You're going to learn to work with your hands, boy. Soon as I get some time I'm—"

"I work with my hands all the time," Brian teased.

"Funny," muttered Mr. Parker. "A man who can't do simple things around the house . . . useless to his—"

"Dad, what did you think when you first met Ma?" Brian asked, cutting into what sounded to be a launch into one of his preachy sermons.

"What did I think?"

"Yeah."

"I couldn't really think . . . she looked so good."

"Love at first sight?" Brian asked, biting into a sausage link.

". . . I wouldn't exactly say that. Then again . . . whatever it was, I knew something had changed for me. Pass me that wrench over there."

"So what did you say to her?"

"Nothing at first. I was with my boys. She was with her girls. We were hustling in the park."

"Hustling?"

"The dance, not a scheme."

"I'm just messin' with you, Dad. Everybody knows about the decade that won't die. You hear it on the radio everyday."

"That's grown folk music," hailed Mr. Parker. "Ay, in the summertime . . . hand me that wrench right there . . . the DJs would set up their equipment in the park. We would go get our friends—didn't have any cell phones back then—and they start calling their friends. Before you knew it . . . the park was crowded and we were jammin'. We'd be out there dancing till we got tired. And when it got late— like ten, eleven o'clock—the cops would come around and tell us to turn the music off. But some of them were cool and told us to just turn it down. Shoot, they were enjoying it, too. You look over there and see them sitting in the NYPD mobile, just chillin'. "

"Y'all were corny."

"Why?" Mr. Parker asked, shifting to the other side. "Fun was fun then . . . and safe. We weren't shooting and killing each other."

"Nah, I mean, dancing in public parks."

"There was nothing else to do. We didn't have computers and videos to sit down all day long looking at. We had to be working, moving."

"So you threw a line on Ma?"

Mr. Parker chuckled. "I just watched her. Let me hold that little round plastic piece over there . . . yeah . . . and I wasn't the only one watching her. She was fine, I ain't kiddin'. A class act . . . especially for that time. And had a body like—"

"You were looking at Ma like that?"

"What! Girl was driving me crazy. Saw her at three different parks before I got up the nerve to even speak. And the way she dressed . . . I had to step up my game."

"You were bumming, Dad?"

"I wouldn't say that. We were all dressing back in the day. But she was . . . *extra*. And she could *do* that hustle. Yep, I'd be moving to the rhythm . . . just watching her feet. Then, one night she was dancing with a buddy of mine. When he spun her around, I broke in. I'll never forget that smile that grew on her face when she turned around and looked at me. We must've danced for an hour straight."

"An hour?"

"Shoot, that was nothing. We could dance till the sun came up."

"That's crazy."

"No it wasn't. We were eating good then . . . had a lot of energy . . . like young people supposed to have. We weren't lazy like your group."

"C'mon, Dad, this is a new day. We're technical."

"Technically full of—"

"Watch yourself pard'ner."

"Ay, what's all this talk about anyway? You messin' around with some girl?"

"Now that really sounds 70s, Dad. I don't mess around. I do the real thing."

"What was that?" Mr. Parker asked."

Brian was laughing. "I'm messin' with you, Dad, relax."

"This is almost done," Mr. Parker murmured, tightening the screw.

"I'm gonna fix you up, Dad," Brian said, preparing their plates.

"That'll work."

It was a rare opportunity for the two of them to eat breakfast peacefully in the dining room while listening to CNN.

BRIAN'S THOUGHTS about Monet prevented him from falling asleep at night. When he tried to change the channel in his mind she only appeared in some other program of his life. She had become his noonday sunshine, his moon at night, and his favorite dessert. He jumped out of bed, grabbed an apple out of the fridge, and went down to the basement to get online.

BryNYshark: What's up? That's how we greet each other here. That's like you would say, how are you doing?

YEMI402: Okay. What's up my friend? I am doing well. There was a film festival in the village today with lessons and activities about HIV/AIDS.

BryNYshark: Cool. Learn anything?

YEMI402: Yes, I learned a lot and there was food and music. We were entertained with dance and poetry. The best part was watching the pretty girls dance. Sometimes I want to take one all to myself. But it goes against my way.

BryNYshark: What is your way?

YEMI402: We are taught by our religion not to get involved until we are married. This is also good because of HIV/AIDS. But many people in my village do not listen and obey their urge instead. This is bad when there is no access to protection and they soon run the risk of dying.

BryNYshark: They tell us the same thing here, but it doesn't stop anything. And they have all the protection they need and still don't use it.

YEMI402: Why is this?

BryNYshark: I don't know, just watch yourself.

YEMI402: I do. I have witnessed too many deaths and I do not choose that for me. It is dangerous because many of the teenage girls here work as prostitutes to support their families and complete their education. And you do not know who they are.

BryNYshark: Word?

YEMI402: Yes, it is word. And some of them are raped and don't ever talk about it or tell anyone. They feel ashamed because of the way we are taught. Are you not a Christian?

BryNYshark: Well, yeah, that's what I was baptized as.

YEMI402: Then you, too, live by the teachings of the church?

BryNYshark: Yes and no.

YEMI402: What do you mean?

BryNYshark: A lot of people go to church, but they don't abide by the rules of the bible.

YEMI402: How is this?

BryNYshark: I don't know. People just do what they want to do.

YEMI402: That would seem to make for a lot of chaos. I thought the American way was civil and moral.

BryNYshark: You'd be surprised. That's why some of our neighborhoods are falling apart.

YEMI402: But you have families, education, and freedom.

BryNYshark: It's like this. Sometimes when you have everything, you take it for granted.

YEMI402: Hard for me to see. It would be a dream to live in America and have so much opportunity.

BryNYshark: I feel you.

YEMI402: I will have to say goodbye for now. It is time for the morning lesson.

THERE WAS nothing more heartrending to Brian than the look in a child's disappointed eyes when deprived of a chocolate chip cookie. Beneath the mask of a clown's happy face at his father's bank's grand opening, he watched the little brown-skinned toddler. Dressed in a pink and purple dress, she bent down to pick up her cookie that had fallen to the ground and was about to put it in her mouth.

"Want to see a magic trick, pretty little girl." Brian asked, distracting her. She was with her sister, who looked to be barely six, and had turned her back to get them hot dogs.

"Get me a couple of cookies," Brian murmured to Ricky, who was giving away balloons. The Cookie Kiosk was a part of the giveaways.

"Can I have a bite of that delicious looking cookie?" Brian asked, rubbing his stomach. "Mr. Happy Clown is sooooo hungry."

The little girl reluctantly handed it over to the colorful character wearing a red wig. She looked so sad as if she were going cry.

"And what is your name?" Brian asked, picking her up.

"Mikah."

"Mikah. What a pretty name. Wanna honk the horn?" he asked and then pressed his fat red nose shooting off an imitation of a cool saxophone riff under his breath.

The little girl laughed. "Go ahead. Honk the horn." When she squeezed his foam nose the classic horn sound went off again, and a fresh cookie appeared in his hand. "See what happens when you honk the horn."

She was a little Monet, sweet, cute, and generous. When she pressed Brian's nose a second time, another cookie appeared in his other hand. In no time he was surrounded by other children, all wanting to honk the horn and receive a cookie.

Standing on his feet for over two hours warranted a break. Brian wandered down the crowded, busy street in

Harlem, and observed the eclectic stores, book vendors, and ethnic eateries amidst the soulful sounds of bootleg CDs. He enjoyed the smiles and stares coming from people, and yet the ability to maintain his anonymity. Passing a subway station he realized he was only a short ride from Monet's fathers' business, where she was working, so he hopped on the train.

THE WEST SIDE Copy Den was printed in bold white on a twin set of royal blue awnings. It wasn't big at all; immaculate and efficiently organized. The fluorescent atmosphere was quaint with friendly advertisements listing the hub of business resources plastered everywhere.

"Can I help you?" A young man asked, studying his appearance. The African American looked smart in the sleek, black rectangular frames.

"I'm looking for Monet," Brian replied.

"Is there something I can help you with?" he asked, almost laughing. "She's assisting another customer."

Monet had been preoccupied with a job collating papers and looked up suddenly. Noticing him, she rushed over in open mouth astonishment.

"How can I help you?" She greeted, as if he were a regular customer.

"Ah . . . I want to inquire about your brochures and flyers."

"Okay, let me see. We have a book over here with all the different samples to choose from . . . based on the kind of product or service you're offering. And the price list," she said, flipping through the pages, "is in the back."

"Got anything for clowns?"

"Pardon me?"

"I've got this idea to start up a clown business, ya dig? You know, where I offer up my services to people looking for some fun in their lives."

Neither of them could resist the comedy and broke out laughing.

"What are you doing here?" Monet asked. "You're supposed to be—"

"I slipped away for a minute," he said, sliding his hands on top of hers. "Just wanted to see you."

"You mean you're still working. How did you do that?"

"I just left."

"Everybody's gonna notice the clown is missing and your father—"

"One of my friends is looking out. I told him I'd be back in a few."

"You'd better get back there," Monet advised, feeling anxious for him.

"What they gonna do?" Brian shrugged.

"That's not the point. You can't disappoint your father like that. What if somebody's looking for you?"

"You worry too much."

"And you take too many chances, so get out of here," she demanded, taking a step back.

"Your father around?"

"No, he's not usually here during—"

"Excuse me, do you have an order for the Thompson group?" asked one of the employees.

"It's on the shelf in the back . . . in two piles. I left it there because I needed to finish— Wait a second," she told Brian, rushing off to find it.

On the counter was the East Side Urban Leaders brochure listing college road trips for the next school year. The regional options included East Coast, West Coast, or the Midwest. Considering the fact that he would be entering his junior year, plans for college wasn't as far away as he'd thought.

"Ya interested?" Monet asked, returning.

"I don't know," he said, perusing its content.

"You have the choice of surfing and sun bathing at one of the top schools in California versus the four seasons in Pennsylvania and Ivy League prestige versus brutal, snowy winters in Chicago. Which one would you like?"

"I say we go to California."

"Oh, you like the heat and the beaches."

"Not just that. You can get far away from your parents . . . and I could sneak into your room at night."

Giggling, Monet dismissed his innuendos and squeezed his fat nose. "You know, I wouldn't mind experiencing it, but I like Pennsylvania. And the University of—"

"Okay, you're missing the point. The idea is to get as far away from here as possible, so I say do the mid-west or west coast college tour . . . even if you decide on one of the east coast schools."

"You're not a good influence, Brian."

"Yes I am and I'll prove it to you when we get there. How much does it cost?"

"For the west cost trip . . . seven hundred dollars. And that's not including meals."

"For a college trip? I could hear my father now."

"It's really not that bad. Three days, flight and hotel."

"When you have it like that, it's not."

"I mean it *is* a lot of money, but it's worth it. Better than spending thousands of dollars and four years of your life only to find out you hate it."

"Is there a GPA minimum?"

"Nope. It says residents of New York City, ages sixteen and up. That makes us both eligible."

"Cool."

"Oh, here it says you need a letter of recommendation from your principal or school counselor. And . . . you have to write a one-page essay expressing your career goals."

"Ah, more work."

"That's easy, though. The hardest part is convincing our parents to let us go."

"You know they're gonna have ninety-nine chaperones, so I don't see the problem. My moms would probably love the idea."

"I think my dad would be okay with it. Speaking of which—" Monet came out from around the counter. "It's time for you to go."

"Now I can see all of you," he said, reaching for her hand. She refused his advance and led him out the door. "Get out, good bye."

"Can I get a kiss?" he asked.

"Brian, go!"

"Please. Just a quick one, right here," he asked, pointing to his right cheek with a fat red finger.

"Not in front of these people, come on," she whispered. "I'm at work."

"Okay, walk with me."

"It's gonna take some time to get back there so go," Monet said, walking hurriedly.

"Nah, the train moves mad fast," Brian told her. "I got here in like ten minutes."

"Still, they could get delayed or something, you never know."

The tenderness in her eyes far outweighed her cautious words when he commanded her gaze at the subway rail. She resisted the urge to wrap her arms around his shoulder and press into his chest. When Brian leaned into her, she welcomed his gentle lips caressing hers in a slow, circular motion that quickly intensified.

"Goodbye," she whispered, noticing the passersby staring at the chocolate girl being kissed by the colorful clown.

"Let me just squeeze you one more time," he asked, refusing to let go.

Laughing, she surrendered to his advances, delighting in several sweet pecks on the lips and then tried to pull away. Holding her tight she stumbled back into Brian's arms and fell helplessly into the affection of his smooth, supple lips.

"That's my girl," he smiled, feeling that electrical surge. He kissed her again and again and backed away feeling dazed. "Let me get outta here," he said and bounced down the stairs.

"You betta," Monet agreed and walked away.

"HELLO."

"Whassup?"

"Who's speaking?"

"Take a guess."

"Brian."

"Oh, so you cheatin' on me wid some dude named Brian. He treatin' you betta than me?"

"Whose this? Wait a minute . . . Brian?"

"Had you going, huh?"

"I knew it was you."

"No you didn't."

"Yes I did," Monet insisted, finding the act amusing.

"Then why are you laughing?"

"Because it didn't sound like you . . . and why are you whispering?"

"I don't want my father to hear me."

"Why not?"

"He whilin' on some craziness, I don't know."

"You got into trouble, didn't you?"

"Misunderstanding that's all. Where are you?"

"Home."

"Doing what?"

"Talking to you."

"Besides that."

"Downloading some stuff."

"When am I gonna see you again?"

"I'll be at work on Saturday."

"I have to wait till then?"

"Okay tomorrow."

"Can't make it. Rules."

"That's right, you've been a bad boy."

"But it wasn't my fault."

"You are funn-ie," Monet giggle softly. "How come you're always getting into trouble?"

"What about Tuesday?" Brian asked, dismissing the 'I told you sos.' "

"I'm working. How about Wednesday?"

"Nope. And Thursday—"

"Wait, I got free tickets to the movies for Thursday," Monet remembered. "My friend works at Soburnes Village Theatre and they show these old movies on Thursdays. Wanna go?"

"What's playin'?"

"I don't know. They change them every week. But you've got four to choose from so I'm sure we'll find something. I love old movies. Do you?"

"Oh yeah," replied Brian, getting excited as he envisioned them in the privacy of darkness.

"We can meet at Stellano's, sneak in a pizza sub or something."

"And sit in the back so I can get my kiss on."

"I'm hanging up," Monet threatened.

"No, no wait. I'm just messin' witchu."

"Are you coming or what?"

"I'll be there, yeah, but I wanna ask you somethin'?"

"What?"

"You gonna let me squeeze up on you a little bit?"

Click.

seven

From: Brian Parker"
To: "Yemiate Bekele"
Subject: Shaft in Africa

I saw this old movie from the '70s tonight called **Shaft in Africa**. I was surprised to see that it was filmed in Ethiopia. They hire this African American detective dude named Shaft to infiltrate the European slave cartel that's kidnapping your people and bringing them to Europe to work. They have them doing hard labor in factories and farms, road gangs and kitchens while they stashing all the profits. Similar to the slavery that happened in America.

Shaft is a bad dude, yo. He penetrated their whole game and got to the man at the top, fell in love with this African

American princess whose brother had been killed trying to stop the cartel, and lived happily ever after.

I was surprised to see how developed Addis Ababa is. It looks similar to what a city over here looks like with cars and buses. The only difference was people were speaking your language. Oh, and in the small villages I saw people riding camels. You ever rode one?

Who knows, I might pop up in Ethiopia one day. I guess that would be just as much a miracle to see me over there, as it would be for you to come over here.

Funny, I felt this connection watching the movie. Maybe it's because I've been talking to you. Let me ask you something. Do the women in your country run around topless like that for real? I was watching the movie with my girl so I had to be cool, feel me? You got to go to a strip club to see something like that over here. LOL! (That means laugh out loud.)

I'm glad to know you, man. I'll reach out to you soon.

Peace

BRIAN COULDN'T stop yawning after eating a number five breakfast special he'd purchased at Brogan's Coffee Shop the next morning. Half the sausage, egg, and cheese hero was gone before he arrived at school. By the time he walked into his second period class the hash browns and orange juice had been devoured. Before delving into his science report in the computer lab, he checked his email.

From: "Yemiate Bekele
To: "Brian Parker"
Subject: "Our School"

Bad news has come to the village today. The funds for the school did not come through. Everyone is so disappointed, the children more than the men who were hired to build the school. It is a huge letdown for them as well. They needed the work in order to feed their families. I will say good bye for now.

BRIAN FELT uneasy for the rest of the day sensing Yemi's disappointment. When school ended he went to Telham Park's public library and surfed the web for information about Ethiopia—the history and culture in particular. Sitting alone, in an atmosphere of abundance—complete with books, magazines, computers, videos and furniture—he wondered why. Why the persistent and unceasing poverty in a historically rich country? Why the natural disasters? Disease? Political unrest? And in all of his questions, he thought of encouraging words to offer his friend. The day soon turned into night and Brian waited anxiously to get in touch.

BryNYshark: I got your message today. I'm sorry for you, man. Anything I can do?
YEMI402: I wish that could be possible. Maybe one day.
BryNYshark: Don't give up. Something else will come through. Here we say when one door closes, another one opens.
YEMI402: So many doors have closed for us. Sometimes you feel like there are no doors left and we are the forgotten.

BryNYshark: Never that. There's always hope. At least you have the missionaries there working with you.

YEMI402: They will be leaving us by week's end.

BryNYshark: Wait. Does this mean you won't have the Internet anymore?

YEMI402: They are leaving ten laptops and I will receive one.

BryNYshark: That's great! We can keep in touch. And maybe try to figure something out.

YEMI402: Yes it is great. And I can teach the children and adults in my village how to use it.

BryNYshark: See, that's something positive right there. Keep your head on.

YEMI402: Please understand I have seen the school in my mind so many times and now it feels so empty.

BryNYshark: So what's going to happen now?

YEMI402: There will be no place to go and the children will have to survive as best they can.

BryNYshark: It sounds like school is their livelihood?

YEMI402: Yes, it is a place where they can learn, read and have a meal. As it is, only a few children are able to attend school and even a smaller number for teenagers. I will try as best I can to teach the younger ones reading and math using the dirt as a tablet and a stick to write with.

Yemi's words hit Brian in his gut. Deciding not to break the continuity, he wrote:

BryNYshark: With no family and all, how did you learn to read?

YEMI402: When I was a boy there was an old woman who collected books and read them to me. Some of them were well advanced, but she taught me the alphabet and how to form words. Then, by a miracle she found an old tattered dictionary and I began to study it. Every day I learned a new word and began to form sentences. I lived for that dictionary, sleeping with it as well.

BryNYshark: That's amazing. People here have dictionaries and never use them.

YEMI402: They are very precious to us. The stains of my tears are still in that book. I was reading it on the night my mother died. My bible was in one hand, my dictionary in another.

BryNYshark: What did it feel like to lose your mother?

YEMI402: It did not seem real at first; the emptiness was terrifying. I visit that night in my mind very often. The people in my village sat around a small burning fire weeping silently, some praying, some immobilized by grief. To lighten the spirit the women hummed songs that seem to descend low into the rivers mouth nearby. I laid my mother's stiff body down, placed my head in her breast, and prayed. The tranquil pattering of rain began to fall, hitting the wood in the exact rhythm of my pulsating heart. It was as if it were speaking to me in a song. The elders say that the rain represents the new journey to come. After that it felt as if someone had cut into my heart and separated my soul into many pieces.

BryNYshark: My apologies, man. I didn't mean to bring up bad memories.

YEMI402: Not to worry. My mother is my guiding angel and is with me everyday and at times like this, it is her spirit that I cling to.

BryNYshark: That's why you gotta keep hope alive! The answers are gonna come. Watch and see. I'm gonna get back to you tomorrow.

YEMI402: That would be good. Good bye for now, my friend.

BryNYshark: Later, my friend.

"GIVE ME a line," Brian told Country, taking a seat in the crowded barber shop on Saturday afternoon. "And tighten up the Ceasar."

"Goin' to the car show tonight?" asked Country.

"Nah, you?"

"I might check it out," he replied, swiveling the chair around facing the window. Whatchu been up to?"

"Little bit of everything," Brian replied and caught Christopher coming through the door. "Lightning, what's good?"

"Another day, another win. What's good wit'chu?" Christopher replied, shaking Brian's hand while bumping fists with Country. A portion of his gray sweatshirt was wet from perspiration. "How many heads you got?"

Country looked around taking a quick count. "Seven in front of you."

"Put me on the end of that. I'll be back," Christopher said, walking away.

"Hold up, Lightning," Brian said. "Ay, let me trade places with Nequon," he said, removing his cape. "I'll be back."

"What do you know about Ethiopia?" Brian asked, meeting Christopher outside.

"Ethiopia. A li'l somethin'."

"Like what?" Brian asked, glancing over pedestrian traffic.

"That's what they call Mother Africa, where it all began."

"For Black people, you mean?"

"I'm talking civilization . . . mankind. That's where they found the fossils of 'Lucy' back in the '70s."

"It supposed to be like a million years old, right?"

"That's it," Christopher replied, "and it makes sense. Ethiopia's the oldest state in Africa."

"Okay."

"Islam started to rise from there. And it's huge . . . like twice the size of Texas."

"Right, 'cause most of them are Muslims."

"That's right. And that's where the Falashas are."

"Whose that?"

"The Ethiopian Jews. But most of them live in Israel now."

"You lost me there." Brian was impressed with his friends' depth of knowledge and welcomed the lesson.

"That's a whole nuther curriculum. But it's ironic yo . . . Ethiopia's got civil war . . . they got drought and famine . . . look at all the political tension, yet they were the strongest of all the nations . . . maintained their independence and never got colonized. Even when Mussolini tried to take over, Selassie wasn't havin' it. All of that, but then look at the poverty—"

"On a level we can't even think about," Brian agreed, nodding familiarly. "You be puttin' it down, yo. How you know all of this?"

"I read. I watch—"

Just then Ramel and Joel, two well known graduates of Telham Park High School, who were also part-time entertainment promoters, stopped to hand them postcard flyers before entering the barber shop.

"Whassup?" greeted the tall, dark muscular one of the two, embracing them both. "It's a party for Razi. Come check it out."

"Get there before ten, it's free," said the shorter, dreadlocked one, who sometimes doubled as a DJ, walking into the barber shop. The two were inseparable and they were all about their business.

"I heard this joint is poppin'," Christopher murmured, reading the highlights. "You been there?"

"Nah," Brain replied. " 'Cause we can only get in on Thursdays with the teen crew and I'm not feelin' them. But I don't know, this is a birthday bash for Razi, so you know some of the team gonna show up. Might be worth it to go."

"Maybe," Christopher said, flipping over the postcard. "Maybe not, 'cause Berriman, Taylor, and Walker, live on the west coast."

"Yeah, that's right."

"They're probably using Razi's name to get people in there. He'll stop by at the end, pick up his little cut and keep it movin'."

"You dead on," Brian responded, thinking. "Ay, give me some feedback on this. I met this Ethiopian dude online, right. That's why I was asking you all of this. He's working with this missionary group and they're teaching him how to use computers. So I'm chattin' with him and yo . . . I feel for the brother . . . the things he be telling me is like . . . I never really realized that we have everything over here . . . and they're starving for beans."

"It's crazy," Christopher agreed. "And it's a sad testimony on us 'cause we're not doing anything about it. You gotta figure," he said, pointing his head toward Jeremy's, "what we spend gettin' a haircut . . . could feed a family of five for a week over there."

"That's real. And since I met this dude, my head's been spinnin', yo. He's mad smart. Speaks different languages. Well, they may not be languages, but whatchu call that when they speak um—"

"Dialects."

"Yeah, dialects, that's it. And right now, his biggest dream is to go to school . . . in a uniform . . . with some books . . . and a toilet. You believe that?"

"And look at these knuckle heads over here . . . throwing it away," Christopher said.

"And check it, he told me it costs ten thousand dollars to build a school."

"Word?" Christopher asked, a questionable frown growing.

"Yo . . . I mean it wouldn't be a state of the art academy like that school that what's his name built, but—"

"Jokas over here'll drop a hunit grand on a piece of ice," Christopher added. "Like that joint Johnny Bee was wearing. You got ten schools right there."

"That's crazy."

"And you got a brother over there who'll give up his right arm just to read a book." Christopher started stretching and continued. "That's the time we're livin' in."

"That's my point. I'm thinking about building a school over there."

"Okay, now you're talkin' with some sense," commended Christopher.

"Where am I'm gonna get my hands on the money is the question?"

"Start with what you got," suggested Christopher. "How much can you come up with?"

" 'Bout a grand . . . and I can probably hit my parents up for a few hundred."

"You'll have to raise the rest."

"How?"

"Put together a fundraiser. With a mission like that . . . you'll get support from everybody. Shoot, talk to Razi."

"Yeah," Brian realized. "He got enough money to bankroll the whole knot."

"I wouldn't depend on him like that . . . gotta always have a plan B. Throw a party and let Ramel and Joel promote it."

"That'll work, too."

"Or you could put on a show . . . or organize a marathon. There's all kinda ways to do it."

"Yeah . . . I'ma think about it," Brian said, shaking Brian's hand. "I'll hit you up later."

"Aiight, peace."

eight

"This is good," Brian said, whirling the delectable smoothie in his mouth. On his first day out since his privileges had been restored, he took the train into Manhattan and met Monet on Thursday after school.

"Mirky mango's the best," Monet agreed, leading him to a shaded bench against the stone wall that surrounded Central Park. It was bright and sunny outside.

"Oh I'm definitely going back there. Little pricey, but it's worth it."

"Just remember Cortland's with the big C," she said. "It's right across the street from there. Okay, so go ahead. You're want to raise some money for a school and you met this friend—"

"I don't know what it is about him. But when he tells me how poor he lives . . . no mother, no father—"

"That's so sad."

"He sleeps in a hut. Walks like five miles to school, and I don't think he owns a pair of shoes."

"Unbelievable."

"On average they only eat one meal a day . . . sometimes none."

"I know the feeling," Monet said, picking up chucks of mango with her straw. "Not sure if there's gonna be any dinner or not."

"Like you ever missed any meals," Brian smirked, pointing his eyes east at the cluster of luxury high-rise buildings where she lived.

"Huh . . . you'd be surprised. Before all of this, things were different."

Stirring the thick drink Brian looked at her narrowly. "A rags to riches story?"

"You could say that. I remember eating rice and beans or oatmeal some days. And it wasn't because we liked the flavor. There was no money."

Pieces of the puzzle of Monet's life were coming together as Brian pictured her world from humble beginnings.

"And the only time we had meat," she chuckled softly, "was when my mother was able to get temp work in the kitchen at the day care center. They would let her bring home the leftovers."

"You'da never been hungry if I knew you then," he mused, puckering up his cool lips and kissing her cheek.

"Hey, but it's not the worst place to be because . . ." And she pulled a sip of the smooth drink from her straw. "Everything from there is uphill."

"I feel you."

"Really, 'cause think about it. What is life when you can have everything? The joy is in the journey. I mean I look back at those times . . . and I'm grateful . . . and it makes me want to do more."

"You're right." Brian took a sip of his drink and stared into the street watching a procession of NYPD patrol cars go by.

"It's like my mother would always make us finish our homework before dinner," Monet continued. "She said it was better to work on a light stomach because you get lazy and sleepy."

"True story," Brian said, shaking his head thoughtfully.

Monet put her drink down and gazed into the sky at an aerial banner advertising a party cruise line; its title spilling in jagged script. "You want to build a school in Africa, huh?"

"Yeah, I do."

"I can see that."

"So can I . . . with ten grand."

"That's not so bad."

"It's not like millions . . . but it's a lot for me."

"I collected two thousand for the church from neighborhood donations."

"How long did it take?"

". . . About a year . . . little longer maybe."

"Okay."

"But there are other ways to raise money that doesn't take as long."

"Fundraisers, right?"

"That too, and then you get your family and friends involved. Ask for donations, put on a barbeque, or a poetry slam, sell T-shirts or—"

"You're beautiful, come here," Brian said, leaning into her.

"I like you, too," she replied and offered him her cheek to caress.

"Come over to my house," Monet asked, and dumped the remaining chunks of the drink in her mouth.

"Now?"

"Let's take the short cut through the park. C'mon."

THE TRANSFORMATION from the noisy urban cityscape into the park's peaceful tranquility and idyllic landscaping was sudden. They stopped along the pedestrian walking trail stealing kisses and hugs between discussions of fundraising possibilities. Coming upon a lake, they watched the ducks float in the water. They stopped and read the schedule of forthcoming performances on the park's SummerStage and continued their stroll toward the east side.

"C'mon, let's make a contribution," Brian said, leading them to the Carousal.

Two dollars per person was a small price to pay for a return to childhood by the steam powered ride. For three and a half minutes the ornate horses and chariots pranced up and down spinning around while the two of them captured glimpses of historic scenery.

Brian was transported into a country fair, watching the trees and benches, taking in the smell of damp grass, and the passing of New Yorkers on bikes. It was three and a half minutes of playful bliss.

They laughed like children when they spotted the middle-aged white man in front of them riding, business attire on and all. He was enjoying the ride just like they were.

"BUT YOU assured me you had it in stock and now you're telling me you don't!" yelled the man as they entered the seventeenth floor condo.

"Daddy!" Monet called out gently to the medium brown figure impatiently pacing the floors.

Brian slowed his steps at the dreamy elegance—the 'Pursuit of Happiness' décor. Vivacious butterscotch, tangerines, and blended browns of linens and cotton glowed like a copper sun.

"Come on in," Monet whispered.

Mr. Kellman eyed Brian like an intruder as he spewed irascible responses. His look and persona reminded Brian of a famous actor.

"Daddy, this is my friend, Brian."

"Nice to meet you, sir," Brian greeted, extending his hand to the skeptical patriarch. His grip was strong, almost intimidating.

"Yes, but I asked for five color screens," he charged, sharply turning away. Aside from his low-cropped hair and goatee, Monet was the female version of Mr. Kellman. Taller than Brian by a few inches, he was handsome, yet looked like the kind of man that doesn't mind getting his hands dirty and lives by his instincts. "What school do you go to?" he asked suddenly, closing the call.

"Telham . . . Telham Park."

"Where's that?"

"Brooklyn."

"Long way from home."

"He's volunteering at the church, Daddy, and he's such a good worker."

"Is that right?" Mr. Kellman nodded, giving him a man-to-man once-over. "Good help is hard to find."

"He's one of those techno-guys who goes to computer camps and can write software," she told him, blinking at Brian. "I met him coming from the geek conference."

"Okay, okay."

"This is nice," Brian commended, his eyes scanning the fine furnishings and the spectacular view."

"Um hum," he grunted. "Have a seat."

Brian set on the comfortable chaise and ran his hand over the velvety throw. He glared into the electric wall mounted copper fireplace thinking.

"Excuse me sir, when did you start working for yourself?"

Narrowing his eyes, Mr. Kellman summoned his recollection as if Brian had asked an important question. "Always did, now that I think about it. Started selling

Kool-Aid . . . no, it was iced tea. My mother would make a big pitcher of it and I would go door to door selling a glass for a nickel."

"Look at all the companies today making millions off of iced tea."

"And if she were alive . . . she'd be one of them." Mr. Kellman rested the papers in his hand and continued. "Then it was Kool-Aid, then on to bicycle rides."

"Bicycles?"

"Yeah," Mr. Kellman chuckled, almost breaking a smile. "Ten cents a ride."

Monet was laughing. "Every time he tells me that story it cracks me up, because that is so my father. He finds opportunity in everything."

"What's wrong with that," he asked and then joined Monet laughing, which sounded more like he was grunting. Soon they were all laughing.

"Okay, so what do you like the most about working for yourself?"

"The challenge." Mr. Kellman didn't even have to think about his response. "Everyday is new, the headaches, too . . . but it's the chance to make more that drives you."

"Tell him what you don't like about it?" Monet asked, looking through some of his papers.

"Employees," he replied, and then his phone rang. "Not easy to come by. Not the good one's anyway. Excuse me, let me take this."

"I think he likes you," whispered Monet.

"Why wouldn't he?" asked Brian. He was being facetious.

"Dad doesn't like anybody. Of course I rarely bring anybody home."

Except for the gene lines and complexion, Monet bore little resemblance to Mrs. Kellman, who posed in a close head and shoulder portrait on the mantle. At her age, she was still a fox with gorgeous hair, pretty brown eyes, and a sexy smile.

"I want to meet your mother," Brian said.

"She's in North Carolina with my grandmamma, but she'll be back on Wednesday."

"Is that an invitation?"

"You're welcome here anytime," said Mr. Kellman from the kitchen. "Where's your manners?" he asked Monet. "Offer our friend something to eat."

Brian winked at Monet, clearly conscious of his winning personality and the effect he had with people. He had scored again and he knew it.

YEMI WAS on Brian's mind. Daunted by the immeasurable poverty drawn by his words, Brian envisioned a young man of his own kind walking miles in sweltering heat hoping to find food and water. Praying without cease to someday get an education without a mother or father present in his life was unfathomable in Brian's thinking. He hadn't heard from Yemi in almost a week and reached out on Thursday afternoon and found him online.

YEMI402: The missionaries have gone. I work on my lessons late into the night when I can.
BryNYshark: What time do you usually go to sleep?

YEMI402: I do not look for sleep because it is hard to rest when so many children are crying and the adults are coughing. This is because they have not had much to eat and have become ill. And then I am on watch keeping the wild animals away.

BryNYshark: You can see the animals from your window?

YEMI402: We do not have windows in our huts. They are very small and made of wood and clay. There is just enough room for my straw cot where I rest and a place to cook.

BryNYshark: Have you eaten?

YEMI402: Not today.

BryNYshark: You alright?

YEMI402: The men went out hunting. Food may come soon.

BryNYshark: Hang in there.

YEMI402: Pray that I can.

"YOU DON'T have much of an appetite tonight, Brian," Mrs. Parker observed, turning off the evening news. The mountain of pasta with meatballs, a garden salad, and a basket of garlic bread had hardly been touched. "Had a big lunch?"

"Not really . . . it's just a lot of food."

This was Brian's fourth opportunity at a meal today; he had been counting. Yet Yemi didn't eat as many meals in a week, none probably as substantive in a year. By refusing food, or not eating as much of it, allowed him to imagine hunger. If he could abstain for an entire week and really feel hunger's wrath, he might be rewarded with a resolution. That's what he was thinking.

"Ma, do you realize most Americans are overweight? I think they just eat to be eatin'; they're not really hungry."

"That's right," Mrs. Parker agreed.

"And you got people in other parts of the world starving."

"You don't have to go around the world, Son. You got hungry and homeless people right here."

"Yeah, but you can always get on a soup line or go to a food pantry. People in third world countries . . . they just die."

"Unfortunately, that's true."

"I never realized how much food *really* means. Like children don't grow without food. Or their brains don't develop and . . . and their immune system . . . just breaks down."

"That's Yelverton Benjamin alright."

"Talkin' about Grand Dad?"

"You remind me so much of him sometimes," she said sitting down. "Just as stubborn . . . did what he wanted to do but he'd give you the shirt off his back. Couldn't stand to see anybody hungry . . . especially children. Always giving stuff away. Used to drive my mother crazy."

"You think that's me?"

"Do I think?" she chuckled, looking into his dark brown eyes. "Your middle name is Yelveron and you're just like him. When you were a baby . . . you were never selfish. When other kids wanted some of your food or wanted to play with your toys, you'd just hand them over."

"Evening family," greeted Mr. Parker, entering the kitchen loaded with office supplies.

"What did I do to deserve you?" Mrs. Parker said, rapping her arms around him.

"How's it going, Brian?"

"Good."

"Sure?"

"Yes," Brian replied, reading one of his technology magazines. "I'll be right back," he told his parents and headed upstairs.

"You think something's wrong with him?" Mrs. Parker said, glancing at Brian's untouched plate. "I can hardly get him to eat these days."

"That girl's on his mind."

Mrs. Parker cocked her freshly arched brow inquisitively and set the partial portion of pasta she was preparing down. "What girl?"

"I don't know who she is," he replied mindlessly, sifting through the mail. "I see him workin' out, cutting his hair. You know the signs."

"Think he's losing his appetite?" she queried uneasily. "Calvin, you don't think he's—"

"I'm not sure," he murmured preoccupied with a bill he'd received. "That love bug plays tricks on a boys' mind." He tossed the mail aside and then planted a sincere kiss on her silky forehead. "But I'll find out. I'm gonna let him have his toys back."

"I NEED some extra hands, Joel said to the male volunteers in the kitchen at United Front Episcopal. He was one of the drivers of the tractor trailer that transported food throughout the north east and mid west. Out of the three males available, Brian was the youngest and possibly the strongest. Running almost an hour late Joel was in a mad rush to unload the fifty-three footer. The line of people outside was already extending around the corner, and it was starting to drizzle.

"Where'd you get this load from?" Brian asked.

"Pennsylvania. Supermarket chain donated it."

There had to be three hundred or more cases of dry goods and canned foods, bottled water and juices packed in the tractor trailer.

"I'm gonna get a couple of those guys on line to help," Brian told Joel. He grabbed the first five who appeared to be able to carry the weight.

Carrying sometimes two cases at a time, Brian must have made about ten trips. He felt an obligation to perform at his maximum in the presence of the less fortunate and downtrodden, many of whom were former drug addicts or mentally ill. Some of them weren't physically strong as they'd once been, and Brian could see them struggling with the heavy loads.

A half an hour had passed by the time the truck was emptied, leaving Brian feeling the exuberance of a strenuous workout. Coming out of the men's room he walked past the chapel and noticed it was empty inside. Drawn into the calm of the devotional space, Brian walked down the center aisle, sat in the front row pew, and looked at the stained glass window. Inside of the colorful glass were glowing works of art; images of ordinary people enclosed by a pair of wings and the words written at the bottom read 'Angels of A Kind.' In the quiet, Brian reflected on his thoughts and felt the presence of peace inviting him to honestly express himself.

GOD, I'm thinking seriously about helping these people—who are really my people. Well I don't have it explain it to you, you already know. Am I losing it or are you calling me to do this? If my thoughts are irrational, tame the anxiety in me. If you're calling me to do this, show me the way. Maybe that's the reason I'm here in this church feeding the homeless. Wish I could give some of this food to Yemi. It feels good when you know people are full and satisfied. Is it true that there are no coincidences?

Brian was still for several moments waiting for a response from a source greater than him. A simple yes or no would suffice. A go this way or that would have been helpful. A step by step guide for what he aspired to do would be more than a gift. Brian received none of those, and was left to his own conscious.

"THIRTEEN HUNDRED and twenty nine dollars," he said, reading the balance of his bank account on line. It was his personal stash from money he'd received from birthday and holiday gifts over the last few years. "I could use this now and make it up later," he said and then remembered the money his parents had put away for his college savings. Feeling hopeful, Brian picked up the phone and called Monet.

"Excuse the interruption of your evening meal. I have a special announcement from the other side of town."

Monet laughed.

"I'm pulling all my resources together and I think I can come up with the money."

"Really?"

"Well, I'm thinkin' I can get my parents to match what I've got and then— Ay, you think your father would get up off of some of his loot?"

"For a cause like this? Sure. *And* you could solicit donations from the neighborhood."

"True."

"Put together a website," Monet suggested. "But then you have to drive people to it and everyone doesn't have computer access."

"Enough of them do. And I can get my boys to help me on that."

"Hey . . . every penny counts. Wait, let me take this call. I'll call you back."

It was time to consult Integrated Vision about his plans. Malyck was the first one of them to return his call.

nine

"WE ARE now faced with the fact, my friends, tomorrow is today. We are confronted with the fierce urgency of now. In this unfolding conundrum of life and history, there is such a thing as being too late. Procrastination is still the thief of time. Life often leaves us standing bare, naked, and dejected with a lost opportunity. The "tide in the affairs of men" does not remain at the flood; it ebbs. . . ."

Brian was held captive by Martin Luther King, Jr.'s brilliant oration about the Vietnam War. There are no coincidences, he realized. He was meant to be in the media room of the library with the debate team at that exact moment to be in earshot of the profound words of the civil rights leader.

"Now let us begin. Now let us rededicate ourselves to the long and bitter—but beautiful—struggle for a new world. This is a calling of the sons of God, and our brothers wait eagerly for our response. Shall we say the odds are too great? Shall we tell them the struggle is too hard? Will our message be that the forces of American life militate against their arrival as full men, and we send our deepest regrets? Or will there be another message of longing, of hope, of solidarity with their yearnings of commitment to their cause, whatever the cost? The choice is ours, and though we might prefer it otherwise we must choose in this crucial moment of human history. . . ."

Martin Luther King, Jr.
Vietnam Speech

"You heard the man!" exclaimed Christopher, as members of the debate team applauded.

When the lights came on inside the media room Brian approached Christopher. "Jordan told me you were here, what's good?"

"Trying to get motivated. Whassup witchu?" he asked, embracing his friend.

"Got a earful, yo. That's what . . . forty somethin' years ago," he said, referring to Martin Luther King, Jr.'s words, "and he sounds like he talking to us today."

"It was the message to the young warriors," Christopher nodded in agreement, " 'cause they were doing they thing, ya dig?"

"I feel you," Brian replied. "Ay, when you get a minute, I need to talk." Catching a glimpse of urgency in his eyes Christopher excused himself and walked Brian to an empty table in the corner of the library.

"This thing is eatin' me, yo . . . tryin' to do this show—"

"Oh, for the fundraiser, so whatchu got?"

"I talked to Jenkins the other day," Brian said. "Too complicated to try to do it here. Gotta get permission from this one, that one. Then they want verification from the organization 'cause you're sellin' tickets."

"What about doing something outside . . . in the park?"

"I checked that out already. You gotta fill out an application, pay all these fees . . . and then you gotta reserve the time way in advance. I want to do this now. At least sometime before I go to the camp in the summer."

"You workin' on high speed, yo. The real world ain't rockin' on instant."

"I don't know, the way I see it . . . you turn up the heat the water's gonna boil quicker."

"I feel you, so where we at?"

"Nowhere right now. I got the idea to do a show, but bringing it together, finding the talent—"

"You can get that right here. Turn it into the *Telham Park's Got Talent* competition or just a night of entertainment with some local people performing."

"That's different."

"Yo, you could put the school choir on stage," Christopher suggested. "They're winning awards all over the city."

"But that's a lot of people to pull together. I want like . . . R&B acts or rappaz, maybe a comedian, you know, talent that's gonna hit the audience hard. And they have to be people I can depend on, 'cause they're not gettin' paid for this . . . so you know how that is."

"What about Rockmon?"

"Nah . . . can't trust him. He might bust up in there with a blunt in one hand and a forty in the other thinkin' he's sittin' at home watching a live show on TV."

The two of them started laughing.

"Even when he's high," said Christopher. "That dude is funny, yo. Remember that time we were all in the park behind the mall? It was right after Labor Day 'cause we had just started school."

"Yeah."

"Yo . . . that dude was so high he thought the girl's baby carriage was a chair and tried to sit in it."

"That's like the night we were coming from the game at school, and he jumped on the top of Tommy's ride, ayo—" Christopher buckled over in laughter and struggled to get the story out. "Tommy forgot he was up there and took off. Rockmon was holding on like batman, and you could see he was scared."

"He crazy," Brian laughed. "We can't have that. Ay, but what about the Urban Violins?"

"That'll work, if you can get them. "You said you want single acts, how about Isaiah? The poets? Ay, and Jordan can be your comedian."

"Yeah, he's good."

"And Kenya."

"Kenya Robinson? If we could get her, yo . . . it's over."

"All you gotta do is ask. Oh, and my man um . . . Gilroy."

"Whose that?"

"He lives in my building. Goes to Washington."

"Performing Arts?"

"Yeah. Ay, this cat can do some things with a horn that'll make you stand at attention."

"Ah man, throw some jazz up in there . . ." Brian got excited thinking of the variety.

"There's your show right there."

"I can see that."

"And maybe you can give some local no names a shot. Everybody wants to get on stage. And then they'll bring their friends and family."

"That means more ticket sales," Brian said thinking, a film of a sold out concert passing vividly over his mind.

"Let's make it happen."

"Stay tuned." Brian said, slapping hands with Christopher. "I'ma catch up witchu later."

"IT'S THE ONE and only. TGIF!" Brian happily greeted, entering the house and heading upstairs. The weekend had officially begun and he had plans, and they were major.

"Ma, what's goin' on?"

When Mrs. Parker responded weakly, Brian redirected his course to the kitchen. Despite the savory aroma of home cooking, the steely aura hit Brian immediately. Mrs. Parker was tossing a garden salad. Mr. Parker was seated at the table, still and expressionless.

"I didn't know you were here, Dad." What's the matter?"

"Disappointed," Mrs. Parker replied softly. For the congenial woman who had an encouraging perspective on everything, the sadness in her voice sounded strange. And for the house that was particularly lively on Fridays: old school jams on the radio, food and laughter with family or friends, it was unusually quiet.

"What happened?" Brian asked, hoping he wasn't responsible for the look on his father's face.

"Issues at work," she responded slicing cucumbers.

"Like what?"

"You know that position your father was trying to get?"

"The analyst, yeah."

"They gave it to somebody else."

"As hard as Dad worked for it!"

"He had already planned the celebration," she muttered solemnly. "It was supposed to be a surprise . . ." Wiping her hands she exhaled slowly, wearing a look of defeat. "What can you do?"

"Find another job, that's what you do."

She smiled at Brian's naivety. "If only it were that easy. Your father's lucky to have a position the way companies are downsizing or going bankrupt. Looks like he's gonna have to sit tight for a minute."

"That's not right!"

"Life's not always fair, Son."

Mr. Parker was as still as a doorknob as he peered out the window. Brian recognized that expression from adults' faces headed out in the mornings to go to work. It was a strained mask that hardly cracked a smile.

Mr. Parker wanted out of his job and into his own business since he retired from the military. His parents had planned to build a real estate business and they agreed that Mrs. Parker would obtain the broker's license and he would support her efforts until the business could stand on its own. That was the dream.

Brian had sensed that his parents' finances were growing lean when he saw his mother doubling her efforts to create multiple streams of income, and his father working longer hours. And neither of them were denying Brian anything in the process. The eat-in kitchen table shrunk in size, appearing too small for the large man leaning on his propped hands. For the first time he empathized with his father's disappointment.

"So we've got what we need for now." Mrs. Parker said removing the chicken out of the broiler. "Doing better than a lot of people out there."

"C'mon Dad, it's a small thing to a giant. That's what you're always telling me."

"That's right," Mrs. Parker agreed, turning the chicken quarters over one by one.

The classic old world clock on the wall chimed melodically, now at the half-hour officially calling it evening. Brian rested his gaze on the swinging pendulum. The clock had been a housewarming gift from his father's friend Cameron. He remembered the day they received it and how beautiful Mrs. Parker thought it was.

"I'll give you five years the most to hang here and we'll be on to bigger things," Mr. Parker said when she mounted it on the wall. It had been seven years and the dream had not been realized. Not the fine estate he'd hoped to purchase, a summer home, and the luxury vacations at least twice a year.

C'mon Dad, let's see what's happening in the Wall Street Journal, he wanted to say, something that he knew his father loved to do, but then remembered the huge amount of money he recently lost in the stock market. *Let's shoot up to the house in the Pocono Mountains where we can fish would have been a good suggestion.* Only after falling victim to the retirement fund scam and much of his 401K had been lost, his father decided to let that house go. The greatest challenges hit when you're closest to your victory, was one of his father's famous sayings. *And then I haven't exactly been a shining star in his crown either.*

Okay, what if I told you I'm gonna do what no sixteen year old in Telham Park has ever done before? Take on a project and change people's lives on the other side of the world. You wouldn't believe it, right? No Dad . . . it's not a scam. You'd be so proud it would make your toes curl . . . another one of your famous sayings.

Mr. Parker stood up and walked over to the cabinet where he stored his alcohol beverages and pulled out a bottle of vodka. "Got any cranberry juice?" he asked Mrs. Parker, pointing his eyes toward the refrigerator.

"Mmm, I know there's some apple juice in there," she replied. "I see some grape juice, but I know you don't want that." Assisting him, she reached for a cocktail glass and said, "Look in the closet."

Mr. Parker pulled out a bottle of white cranberry juice from the pantry. He took a sip of the drink he'd mixed, testing the flavor, and then laced it with another serving of vodka.

"You alright, Dad?"

Mr. Parker took a healthy gulp of the mixed cocktail, slid the bottle aside, and walked away. "I have to be alright, Son. I have to be."

IT WAS well after 2:00am when Brian heard the front door open. He leaped out of his desk chair and hurried out of his room. Mr. Parker had been out all night and hadn't told his mother where he was going, and the car was still in the driveway.

Mrs. Parker leaned over the banister relieved that her husband had made it home and decided to let the two men in her life have a moment.

"Aaaay!" Mr. Parker looked happy and glassy-eyed in his inebriated state. "Come here," he said, pulling Brian close. He kissed his forehead reeking of alcohol and judging from his awkward footing, he had plenty of it. "You know you my boy, right?"

"C'mon Dad, it's late. Time to go to bed."

Drinking had the opposite effect on Mr. Parker's personality. He was a kind, loving, and gentler person, as if he had traded places with someone else.

"Any dinner left?"

"Yeah Dad, but it's too late to eat, C'mon" he urged, afraid his father might be going to the cabinet for another drink.

Humming, he leaned his weight on Brian with awkward coordination and stumbled on the stairs. Planting himself comfortably on the steps, he shook his head sadly.

"Where you're headed, son . . . it's not easy. I tried to soften the blow . . . give you a little head start. But look at me . . . hard being a man." Mr. Parker laughed a drunken man's cry and pulled Brian down next to him. You know I love you."

"Yeah, Pops."

"I bet you don't know how much I love you."

"Yes I do. C'mon Dad."

Mr. Parker laughed again. "Love you better than I love myself, boy."

"I know Dad, I know."

Mr. Parker's sentiments weakened Brian as he helped him up the stairs. After his father was safely asleep, Brian reached out to Yemi.

BryNYshark: Something's come over me and I want to take this project on. It's a lot of hard work, but I can change people's lives. I'm just not sure I can do it.

YEMI402: If it is a vision, there can be no fear.

BryNYshark: What's the difference between a dream and a vision?

YEMI402: I think in a dream you see images of what you hope for swimming in your mind when you are sleeping or sometimes awake. What you see in a vision comes from somewhere divine and is greater than you.

BryNYshark: I want to do it, but I don't know where to begin.

YEMI402: If what you saw is purposed for you there will be a way made. You will be divinely directed and all the people you require will appear to assist you.

BryNYshark: Thanks man. I'll say it again. You're a smart dude Yemi.

YEMI402: If you say I am smart, I wish to be smarter. In the way school helps you to be smart.

BryNYshark: School's gonna happen for you one day. I can feel it.

YEMI402: I hope your feeling is right. We will talk again soon.

BryNYshark: Here we say: Keep Hope Alive!

YEMI402: Keep hope alive, my friend.

"FIVE TEENAGERS from the south side of Telham Park were killed on Wednesday evening," Christopher read out loud in the barber shop Thursday afternoon. "Their bodies were found in an abandoned apartment and their heads were covered with plastic."

"It's been all over the news," added Brian, who had dropped by after leaving the game room with Ricky.

"It was a nasty scene," a guy they called Lucky who worked with Country said. "I saw them bringing them out of the house in body bags. That was one of Derk's cousins, my man Lenny's boy, and I was in the car with him when he got the call so we went by there. Thank God for every day," he nodded. " 'Cause you don't know when your time is up."

"Umm hum, that's right," mumbled Tin Mars, sweeping the floor. The recovering addict was once a solidly built, healthy working man prior to his wife being murdered. Unable to cope with the grief he fell into the claws of drugs and alcohol. After suffering several seizures he chose to live, and underwent rehabilitation. The talented artist sold paintings on the boulevard in the daytime, and for a few extra dollars and some company, he cleaned the barbershop in the evening.

"They were so young," noted Christopher.

"That dude they call Steel . . . yo, they had to restrain his mom's," Lucky remembered.

"How many teenagers you think are living in Telham Park?" asked Brain, abruptly switching the subject.

"Two, three thousand," replied Lucky, taking a wild guess.

Betta for them to be at a show than on the street, yo. You gonna work it out or what?" Christopher asked. "Lotta idle minds out there."

"It's a lot to put together," Brian said. "I need a team. Somebody to—"

"You could start right here," Country jumped in. "Give everybody a part to play and recruit all them knuckleheads out there that don't have nothin' to do."

Brian nodded, thinking, but a loud crash startled him.

"Didn't I tell you that was gonna happen?" said Lucky, who was the first to get to the window. "The way those cars race through that stop sign, I knew it!"

A Hispanic man got out of the SUV whose front was smashed and ran over to the demolished car to see if anyone had been injured. He pounded on the window but the man's head was down and he didn't respond.

"Don't tell me that dude is dead," said Christopher.

"We'll find out in a minute," said Country as he watched his customers rush outside to the scene.

"It's a crazy day," said Brian suddenly feeling anxious. "I gotta hit this store before it closes," he said, remembering to pick up his mother's suit from the tailor's downtown.

By the time Brian walked to the bus stop, the police had already blocked off the street and detoured traffic in another direction. Buses were nowhere in sight and Brian decided to walk the fifteen block stretch.

Two dumpsters sitting outside of the old movie theatre on Brazelton Avenue drew Brian's curiosity as he passed by. He hadn't seen those doors open since he was a kid, when his feet were unable to touch the floor. Three men came out loaded with garbage and debris and that's when Brian peeped inside. Seeing into the gigantic lobby brought on memories.

"How ya doin'?" Brian said to one of the gentleman hauling out materials. He was a big, dark, middle-aged man.

"Good," he replied. "How can I help you?"

"Just looking around," Brian said, sizing up the space. "Need some help? I can't do it right now, but—"

"No thanks," he smiled. "We're good."

"Y'all gettin' ready to open up somethin'?"

The man looked over the inside as if he were thinking. "This is gonna be the new home for First John Baptist."

"Wow. You can hold a lot of people up in here."

"We're hoping to have a big congregation."

"You're a member of the church?"

The man took off his right glove and offered his hand to Brian. "Reverend Monday, and you are?"

". . . Brian. This is your church?"

"For seventeen years now."

Brian followed the man further inside talking. Everything was still in the old theatre just as he'd remembered it.

"I used to come here when I was a kid."

"Is that right?"

"Looks smaller now."

"That's because you grew up."

"It seemed like thousands of people were here when I was little."

"Not quite. Including the balcony it holds a little over six hundred."

Through the interior doors you could see the seats and the stage. It smelled of mold and years of neglect but its potential was apparent. The men inside were breaking down chairs. "Doesn't look bad. What are y'all gonna do with all these chairs?"

"Throw them away."

"They're old and worn," he told them.

The room suddenly came alive in Brian's mind. *New seats. Bright lights. Booming music and live entertainment.* "I remember that stage," he said, noticing the tattered curtains.

"A lot of famous people have performed here. Then they turned it into a movie theatre."

"How long is it gonna be before it's ready?"

"Oh, a good while. It's gonna take a few weeks just to clean it out. The renovations will probably take about six months or so . . . depending on the contractor."

Brian conversed with the gentleman and thanked him for his time.

From: "Brian Parker"
To: "Monet Kellman"
Subject: My Discovery!

CHECK THIS OUT. The tailor's closing at seven and the street is blocked off so I walk in to the direction of the detour. I see these men bringing all this stuff out of this old theatre that used to rock back in the day. I go in and the new owner is a pastor and he told me they're getting ready to turn it into a church. I leave there and something tells me to go back. I told the Reverend what I wanted to do and asked would it be possible to do a show in the theater before they finish renovating. He told me to put it on paper and he'd review it. I think it's time to talk to my Dad, get him involved and put this show together.

ten

"You can hear him playing from here," noted Brian, walking up the stairs with Christopher to Gilroy's apartment.

"This is every night, yo. We ought to call it Gilroy's Place."

"He's soundin' good."

"Oh, he takes his work seriously . . . and everybody else does, too."

"Sure it's cool coming to the crib unannounced?"

"You wit me," Christopher replied confidently, knocking on the door.

An older gentleman, short, dark and bowlegged opened the door. "Look at my boy!"

"Evening, Mr. Harker? How ya doin' sir?"

"I'm well tonight," he smiled broadly, extending his hand."

"Good, good. This is a friend of mine, Brian."

The strength in the man's strong hand was unexpected. "Good to meet you, sir."

"Mr. Harker . . . um think we could talk to Gilroy for a minute?"

"Him practicing," he replied, sliding his hand down the back of his head. "Don't like interruptions."

"I know but it's kinda important," he explained and caught a glimpse of Mrs. Harker peeping around the door."

"Christ *ee fah!*"

"Hello Mrs. Harker." He was glad to see his sweet Jamaican neighbor. She was shorter than her husband, dark and hefty with a face that glowed when she smiled.

"Why you got the boys standin' *oakside*?" she asked, eyeing her husband. "Him no stranger. Come, come," she said, pulling Christopher into her embrace.

"I got my friend Brian here with me. We need to talk to Gilroy . . . just for a minute."

Mrs. Harker clutched Brian's arm and invited them in. "You boys eat already?"

"Yes we're good," replied Christopher.

Under a spotlight sat bare footed Gilroy in a T-shirt and cargo shorts with a half eaten plate of oxtails, peas and rice with plantains sitting next to him. His smiling eyes acknowledged their presence in his freeform recital that sounded like a mystery film soundtrack.

Glancing over the room Christopher pointed out pictures of Gilroy taken at concerts under soft track lights on the navy blue wall. On an end table were a stack of old vinyl records. "He can imitate every one of these," whispered Christopher, flipping through albums of Miles, Coltrane, Armstrong, and others.

"He's doing his thing," commented Brian, admiring his interjection of dazzling scale work, uniquely tart and sweet with ease and full command.

"Every*ting* cool?" Gilroy asked suddenly, resting his horn.

"Pardon the interruption, man. What's good?" Christopher said, slapping hands with the maestro. "This is a good friend of mine."

"I didn't know, man. I'm sorry." Brian said, clutching his hand.

"About what?" Gilroy's friendly smile was fading.

"I didn't know we had this kind of genius in the neighborhood. This is an honor."

"Not yet," Gilroy smiled. "Come check on me in a few years, what's up."

"Ay, you hooked up this room real nice," Brian commended, looking over the private studio and getting a couple of ideas of his own.

"Makin'due."

"I hear that," said Christopher, anxious to get to the particulars. "Ah, check this out. Brian wants to ask you something 'cause I told him how you and me vibe, know what I'm sayin'. We call him the master tech. Top of his game on that computer. So from genius to genius," he pointed to Brian. "Go 'head, talk to the man."

Gilroy expressed no emotion as Brian spilled out a synopsis of his mission.

"Somethin' just come to me," Gilroy said, and picked up his horn as if he were somewhere else and had not heard a word Brain said. Demonstrating his versatility, in low moans and dizzying romps, he compiled a history of jazz in a lengthy composition and then he rested his horn. "For the children of Ethiopia, you want to build a school?"

"Yeah," replied Brian. "It'll be the first school in the village. See, they're not only starvin' for food; they want an education bad!"

"*Wad de ras* man, like my people *bock* in Jamaica."

"You feel me? So I'm trying to raise the money for the brother, from a brother . . . know what I'm sayin'?"

Gilroy rolled his eyes over toward Christopher, but looked beyond him, a multitude of thoughts evident in his trancelike stare. He nodded slowly and picked up his horn, blew out a more laid-back, silkier, acoustic display of jazz and stopped abruptly. Bowing his head he said, "Sorry mon, I didn't know."

Brian glanced at Christopher, who was stroking a hand thoughtfully over his chin.

"I didn't know we had this kind of consciousness in the neighborhood," Gilroy said in words classically designed in American English. He could turn his accent on and off on a whim. "I'll play for you anytime."

A smile of wide proportions lit up Brian's face.

"I told you he's was the man!" remarked Christopher, almost laughing.

"That's platinum *tinkin'*," Gilroy said shaking Brian's hand. "Powerful," he added, and without missing a beat he unleashed a part of his musical identity in a solo bristling with warmth and depth.

On that note Christopher and Brian made their exit.

"GIVE ME a hand," Khalid asked Brian, pointing his eyes toward the stack of boxes in front of his house. Jeremy shot past them holding two boxes and a duffle bag. Christopher jumped in to help the duo who called themselves Twin Violins—referring to their instruments, not their biological makeup. At six o' clock Friday evening they were loading up their vehicle headed to Baltimore for a scheduled performance.

"How long y'all gonna be?" Brian asked.

"The weekend," Jeremy replied, glancing at the number of an incoming call on his cell phone. We're playing at the Jazz Fest."

"So I'm sayin', can you play for the show?" Brian asked. They'd been following the musicians for a half hour or better hoping to get them to commit.

"Gotta talk to our manager," said Khalid. He had a welcoming disposition, but when it came down to business the bulky, football player who traded a ball for a bow put his game face on—quick.

"Manager?"

"Nobody's gettin' paid," interjected Christopher. "It's a fundraiser."

"We gotta clear anything we do with our man first," Khalid responded, stacking the boxes of CDs in the trunk of the SUV.

"Alright, but think of all the publicity you gonna get," Brian cajoled.

"That's the bonus," Christopher jumped in, talking to them both. "It's your humanitarian contribution and a little something in it for you, too."

Jeremy wasn't friendly like Khalid, and short on words. He removed a bottle of water from his bag and gulped down a portion. Khalid double checked his pockets and pulled out his ear plugs and tossed them in the SUV thinking on their request.

"Brothers over there won't ever see a violin. Forget about playin' one," Christopher added.

"Play an instrument?" Brian inflected. "My man's gotta hunt for a piece of meat for three days and pray to find some liquid gold that's not contaminated—that's what they call water. See how you takin' it down? Feels good, right . . . keeps you strong. It's not even a thought for you and they're dying of thirst over there. Wrap your mind around that, yo."

"We gotta make this," cautioned the driver on the phone, who was Jeremy's older cousin.

"Do YOU!" Brain huffed, shaking their hands politely. He had known both of them for years and was taken aback by their stiff response.

Khalid jumped into the back seat, Jeremy in the front. Christopher stepped away from the curb thinking. Brian turned away exasperated, taking their indecision personally. "Ay you remember that Rasta dude that does reggae on the guitar?" Christopher asked, crossing the street. "He refused to be—"

"Ayo!" called Jeremy, sticking his head out of the jeep as they pulled off. "What's that date again?"

"It's next month on the 17th," Brian replied.

"I'ma hit you up when we get back. See what we can do." Brian bumped fists with Christopher feeling hopeful. "Aiight, cool."

"Lift every voice and sing,
Till earth and heaven ring
Ring with the harmonies of Liberty;
Let our rejoicing rise . . ."

THE INDUCTION ceremony for the National Honor Society was scheduled to take place at the end of the school year and rehearsals were underway. Members of the prestigious group stood transfixed as Kenya performed the National Black Anthem with Telham Park's high school choir, now for the third time.

The sixteen year old introvert that recently integrated into the mainstream population from special education had become recognized as a rare R&B talent. And after winning the Telham Park's Idol competition several months before, she had become hot property.

"Ever heard any singing like that?" Nadira murmured, standing between Christopher and Brian in the back of the school's auditorium.

Members eagerly applauded as the stylish rendition of the historic composition came to a close and choir members were descending from the stage.

"Pssss, Kenya," Nadira summoned, snaking her way between students as they made their way to their seats. "I need to talk to you."

"What's up," asked Kenya, greeting her in the hallway with a cheek to cheek.

"I was in tears," Nadira squealed. "Where does that voice come from?"

"Get outta here," she said, tossing her hand to the wind. "They asked me to sing for the ceremony so I said let me do a little something different with it."

"What did I tell you?" Nadira said, glancing over at Brian and Christopher. "This girl's a star and everybody wants to get their hands on her now."

"It's the platinum voice," Christopher greeted, embracing her. "How long you gonna keep the world waitin'?"

"How you doin', Chris?"

"Not as good as you. Ay, you know my man, Brian?"

"I'm not really—" And then she paused for a second, gazing curiously. "No, I think I've seen you before."

"Your voice is *whew* . . . incredible," lauded Brian, bringing his hands together praise style.

"Stop that," Kenya blushed, smiling sheepishly. "Thank you anyway."

"When you become famous, can I be your manager?" teased Christopher.

"Too late. She's already got one," hyped Nadira. "Ain't ya heard?"

"Oh it's your time," Christopher said, impressed and happy for her. "And you're ready."

"She was born ready," Nadira declared.

"Well look, we need to talk to you," Christopher began. "My man over here—"

"They want you to sing for this big show they're putting together," Nadira interrupted excitedly. "It's a fundraiser for this project—"

"Would you please let Brian talk," Christopher nudged, cutting her off.

"Go ahead, I'm sorry."

"Okay, I'm putting this show together to raise money for a school I'm building in Africa."

Kenya looked puzzled.

"Okay, I'm working with this missionary organization. They go to Africa and third world countries to teach the poor people and orphans how to read and write, computers and all of that. Right now they're teaching kids outside under trees in that crazy heat. They need books, supplies and the whole nine, so they're trying to build a school."

"That's sounds like something my church is doing," Kenya realized. "They're sending them clothes and money for food."

"Okay, so you know what I'm talking about," Brian said brightly.

"Yeah, I do."

"So what happened was I connected with one of the boys in this village on line, you know, just chattin'. He was the one that turned me on to his missionary group. Said it's like hundreds of children there that want to go to school, but they don't have a facility. So I'm trying to help the missionaries build a school. And that's where you come in. If I can put the talent together, I can sell tickets and raise some money."

"All the proceeds go to the school," said Christopher.

"Ev-e-ry single dime," Nadira emphasized.

"Wow . . . that's big," Kenya remarked, smiling in approval.

"You're gonna do it?" Nadira asked, sounding more like a command than a question. " 'Cause the show will sell out if people know you're singing."

"And this is a serious cause," Brian added coolly. "It's a school to us, a world to them . . . and all you have to do is say yes, share your gift and—"

"How can I not?" Kenya replied joyfully, much to their amazement. "This is a ministry right here, and if you can put together something this extraordinary, I'm with you."

"Praise the Lord!" Nadira hailed, high-fiving the boys. *"It's on!"*

"You're so krazy, Nadira," Kenya said laughing. "I gotta get back in there before they come looking for me," she said backing away. "Oh, so where's it gonna be and what day—"

"We'll give you the details when we get it all together," Brian assured her warmly.

BRIAN COULD feel his stomach expanding drinking a quart of spring water before his morning workout. He shivered slightly as the cold liquid circulated his body and headed down to the basement. *Dad, I've been asked to get involved with this project in Africa. No . . . Building a school in Africa has to be one of the most noble . . .*" While lifting twenty-five pounds on each arm, with very slow and controlled movements, he rehearsed the spiel he would give his father at lunch later on. Students had been given the day off for Staff Curriculum Development and the timing couldn't have been better.

IT WAS BRIAN'S first time visiting his father at work since WG First National moved its headquarters from Manhattan across the river to New Jersey's waterfront. All things were new on the gold coast of restaurants and shopping, pristine architecture and a mix of towering condos. The glass exterior of the commercial high rise gleamed in the noonday sun. Before entering the building he paused at the sight of private yachts along the marina and inhaled a spring's sense of elusive possibilities.

Brian caught a gleam of pride in his father's eyes when he greeted him in the reception area of the 19th floor. They walked through a maze of 8 X 10 cubicles while Mr. Parker made introductions. Everyone was polite and pretended to be happy to meet the boss' kid. He wondered had they all had a disdain for their jobs, feeling trapped and unfulfilled as his father did. Following an extensive tour of the state-of-the-art financial facility, they headed to lunch at the waterfront.

Ordomon's restaurant was full of white linen clothed tables, sparkling glassware, and bay windows. The exhilarating backdrop of the Hudson River and Battery City downtown framed Mr. Parker, who took to reading his financial reports immediately after they were seated.

Looking out into the river Brian gazed at the base of the yacht with bold script reading *Inoir Dream*, which he read like 'In Your Dreams' and thought it was cool. "There's an organization that's into building schools for poor people," Brian said, jabbing into the mountain of lettuce of his chicken Caesar salad. "I'm thinking I want to get involved with them."

"Um huh," Mr. Parker grunted absently, chomping on a turkey club sandwich. He was still reading.

"If I wanted to . . . if I needed ten thousand dollars, where could I find it?"

"What are you talking about? You work for it."

"But what if you don't have that kind of time, and you need the money right now?"

Mr. Parks peered at Brian with blatant suspicion. "What's the rush for ten grand?"

"I'm just sayin'," Brian shrugged. "If some kind of charity or organization needs money to fund a project, what are some other options?"

"Borrow it . . . find an investor . . . get a sponsor."

"What about getting money you don't have to pay back?"

"That's sponsorship. It pays the expenses to do fundraisers. They're grants out there, too."

The glacial presence of the Continental Princess eased into his view, floating across the water with bright-eyed visitors enjoying an afternoon boat ride.

"That's what I need . . . some sponsors," Brian said, fully comprehending the difference. "What do I have to do to get it?"

"What is all this foolish mumbling about?" Mr. Parker asked, the tone of his inquisition bordering on irritation.

Brian knew that the one thing that would send his father through the roof is some half-baked, half-thought-out scheme to do something without adequate knowledge or experience to do it.

"I want to raise some money to build a school in Africa," he blurted boldly.

Biting into the second half of his turkey club, he eyed Brian critically. "A school in Africa?" he mumbled.

"Yes."

Mr. Parker put his sandwich down, wiped his mouth and chewed his food thoughtfully.

"Is everything alright here?" The dark featured Indian waiter asked, already on his second round checking the satisfactory pulse. He was apparently new to the job.

"Everything's good, thanks," Mr. Parker replied, his stern eye pressed on Brian. "Come again with that. What are you saying?"

"I want to build a school in Africa and it costs ten thousand dollars to do it."

"Okay . . . where is all of this coming from?"

"I met a friend online who lives in Ethiopia. He's from one of those villages . . . like the ones we see on television where they're starving, drinking dirty water, and the kids have those protruding stomachs."

"If he's starving, then how can he afford a computer?"

"It came from this missionary group. They went over there with a bunch of those new low powered laptops. I think they cost like . . . a hundred dollars or something like that. They made them for people in third world countries, you heard about it?"

"Yes, I'm familiar. Go on."

"Okay, so I find this dude in the chat room trying to get in touch with somebody in America 'cause he's just learning how to work the net."

"And that somebody just happened to be you?" he asked sarcastically.

"Well . . . yeah."

"When was this?"

"Weeks ago," replied Brian, his eyes chasing the aluminum high-speed boat whizzing by.

Mr. Parker picked up his bottle of Perrier and refilled his glass. "I'm listening."

"Okay, so I get to know him. He's a cool dude. But Dad, they're so poor. They don't have food, schools—"

"It's a third world country."

"Right, so he gets all excited 'cause these missionaries told them that some company was supposed to be building a school for them. He was ecstatic! You would have thought he won a lottery of somethin'."

"Okay."

"Then, like a month later he hits me up . . . devastated now because the company bailed out, couldn't give them the money, and the school is a wash."

"So now *you* want to build a school for your friend?"

"When he told me it costs ten thousand dollars to build a school, with the works, I'm thinkin' . . . that's not a lot of money."

"Is that right? You got that kind of cash—"

"I'm saying Dad, it's not pennies, but c'mon, our cars cost more than that. You always telling me how much those CEOs at the bank spend on these lavish vacations. Their bonuses alone could probably feed . . . entire countries."

"Yes, but they're working people, adults that can—"

"Then those same working people can help support the cause. Some of my friends work, too, or they get money from their parents. You know how much money they spend on—"

"Video games."

"Okay Dad, you're right," Brian conceded, now relating to his father's frustration with frivolous spending. "They throw away crazy money on sneakers, clothes—"

"And they're just gonna make a sacrifice and hand their money over to you? Don't tell me you're thinking about hacking into—"

"I'm not trying to do that," Brian said, cutting him off. "That's why I'm asking you to help me to find a way to raise this money."

Mr. Parker looked at his watch and took another bite of his sandwich. "What makes you think you can pull something like this off?"

"Because I want to, Dad. Look at the impact it'll have in Yemi's village. That's his name. With a real school, they can learn their way out of poverty. I'm telling you this dude gets so hungry sometimes, he can hardly walk. Days without food, Dad, and he never complains. Never! He's hungry right now. Been starving for almost a week and I don't know if he's gonna make it. I could be talking to a dead man."

In an emotional pause, Mr. Parker reflected on Brian's proposal and the passion he exuded for such an enormous undertaking. Either his son had lost his mind or he just woke up to a worthy calling.

"You're always telling me to look at the bigger picture when I'm making decisions, Dad. The picture I see tells me if I can raise this money I can change people's lives . . . for generations to come. Isn't that what it's all about?"

"It is," Mr. Parker agreed.

"And if I can't raise the money, I'm thinking I can use the money from my college fund and then—"

"No, no, you're not touching your college fund. Gotta take care of you first."

"There's a time for sacrifice, that's what you're always sayin'. If it was a matter of life and death, you wouldn't blink."

"But this is different."

"A school can be like oxygen to kids in third world countries, Dad! With an education, they can change their condition. They can eat. They can live."

Taken aback by Brian's mature argument Mr. Parker paused again, this time with the courtesy he would extend to a man his equal.

"I mean, I want to try to raise the money, but if I have access to my own—though I *could* hack into some bank accounts—no I'm just kidding," he teased. "Just wanted to see if you were paying attention, Dad. But look at it this way. I can always work and make the money back, or get a scholarship to go to college. Yemi can't do that."

Mr. Parker gazed at the river. From a distance the two steam boats looked to be threatening collision. "So what organization is this now?"

"Excuse me, finished with that, sir?" The waiter asked.

"Oh the missionary group. They're called Disciples of Change. Now, listen to this, Dad. I got an idea for a fundraising event. I get all my talented friends together and put on a show . . . like a concert. Charge twenty dollars for the tickets and pull in five hundred people. That's ten thousand right there. And whatever I don't make, I'll solicit donations on line, from the community, look for some sponsorship . . . or put in the rest from my own money."

"That'll take a lot of organizing, a lot of time. You'll need some hands that's gonna help you—"

"I've got a team."

"And who's this?"

"Ricky. Christopher. Nadira and her friends. The guys at the barbershop. Integrated Vision."

"And the talent? Where you're gonna—"

"I got them already."

"Who are they?"

Brian went down the list of people much to his father's surprise. "And they're going to do it for free."

"And where's this supposed to take place? You'll need a venue."

"I haven't figured that out yet, but I got this idea."

Mr. Parker was no longer skeptical listening to his son's plan. And the idea of using the old theatre to hold a fundraising event wasn't a bad one. Had he found a cause that peaked his interest, injected within him a sense of purpose and the drive to pull it off? Perhaps all of his preaching was finally beginning to sink in. He looked at his watch, and gestured for the check.

"And Dad, I was thinking. I need you to talk to Razi's uncle and see if he's willing to get up off some of his cash."

"That might be a possibility—"

Mr. Parker looked out into the river, wiped his mouth and hands, and tossed the napkin. "I'll think about it. Let's get out of here."

eleven

*H*i, *you've reached Monet. I'm not available to take your call right now. But if you leave your contact information, you'll hear from me shortly. Be sure and make it a great day, and help someone in need. Toodles. [Beep]*

"What's good? Just wanted to hear your voice. Things are coming together just like you said. I know I met you on that train for a reason. Other than the fact that you're so hot you started a fire in the subway and I happen to be there to put it out. Call me when you get this. Later."

"Brian!" Mrs. Parker called. "You've got a visitor, come downstairs."

An unexpected visitor on a Monday afternoon? Uh oh. The thought of those detectives returning sent Brian flying to the window to see if that blue Dodge was parked outside. It wasn't out there, nor was any other unfamiliar cars.

Brian could hear his mother talking. "Tears came to my eyes watching you at the Highland Classics, boy."

"Lightning, whassup!" Brian exhaled in relief when he spotted Christopher in his kitchen.

"Whassup witchu, man?"

"Survivin'."

"Hope its cool droppin' in unannounced."

"You know you can check on me whenever."

"I just wanted to tell you I talked to Jordan. Told him about what you were doin'."

"What'd he say?"

"Yo . . . he was *beggin'* me to let him be a part of it."

They slapped hands laughing when suddenly, the doorbell rang three times in spends of urgency. Brian caught his mother's astonished glance.

Two visitors in one evening. "Who is this on my bell like that?" Brian said, walking to the door. Looking out of the side window he saw no one.

"Open the door and see," Christopher said, coming up behind him.

Brian leaned to the left and peered through the window.

"Open the door," Mrs. Parker said.

"I want to see who it is first." Brian suspicion was on high alert, particularly in the presence of his mother. "I still don't see anybody."

"Maybe somebody realized they had the wrong bell, Christopher suggested.

"I don't know," Brian said, heading back to the living room. Before he could sit down the ringing came repeatedly.

"Open the door," Christopher suggested. "I'm about to head out anyway."

"You don't have to rush, yo."

"Nah, I've got some things to do, just wanted to holla. Good seeing you Mrs. Parker."

"Don't be a stranger, now."

"Anybody know where Brian lives?" a tall, athletic figure in dark sunglasses asked when he opened the door.

". . . Deshon! That's you! Ahhh, y'all got me good," he grinned brightly, realizing he had been duped. "Whassup?" Brian cackled and embraced him.

"Where you get all this from?" Brian asked, testing his muscles. He was half that size the last time they'd seen him.

"Pumping iron, carpentry, landscaping . . . you name it."

In a T-shirt, jeans, and black and white sneakers, Deshon was a picture of health. "I don't believe it. When did you get home?"

"Friday."

"So good to see you," Mrs. Parker greeted. She hugged the young man that she had so much faith in tight and they swayed from side to side.

"But I just saw you yesterday," said Brian.

"Seems like it, right. But it's been a few months."

"How you doin', man?" Brian asked, hugging him again.

"I'm good."

"Sure do look good," added Mrs. Parker. "Let me get y'all something to drink."

Brian was looking at a different Deshon. Not the hotheaded, cocky fireball ready to rip off a dude's head on a dime. Fighting with the Shadows, a local street gang, he had been fearless. Yet his real friends called him the future architect; he could build anything. Deshon wasn't wearing his earring either. The one he took off before beating a rival unconscious. The altercation began in the bleachers during football skirmishes at the Telham Park field. Deshon stepped to one of the neighborhood girls and tapped her on the butt, a subtle way of claiming his familiarity with her.

The 'bling' wearing gangster, also known as G Rod, was offended and the two of them exchanged words. Deshon had been drinking beer—maybe something else in the way of smoke or other drugs that had been passed around—and he feared nothing.

When they faced off Deshon turned his back to remove his earring with the delicate savvy of a girl, and dared him to sneak one up on him, but since he didn't take the opportunity—*pow*! Deshon surprised him with a right uppercut. The young man was out cold. That was his first year of high school. Moving with street gangs wasn't the move for the son of a correction officer. But thankfully—and because of his father's position and his clean record—after defending himself against his gang rival, the judge was lenient and sentenced him to ninety days in a boot camp.

"What's happening on the Ave?" asked Deshon. "Everything's changing. The Frontier is gone."

"They were competing with Rodell's," said Christopher, "and their jerseys and hats were over the top. Nobody's spending that kind of money on clothes right now. Economy's tight."

"Captain Rigby's went out of business, too," Brian added. It was everybody's favorite fish house.

"So whatchu been up to? Still hackin'?" Deshon asked. He was being facetious.

"C'mon, I don't do that any more," Brian laughed. "But I'm glad to see you, man. You're just in time."

"For what?"

"I can use your building skills right about now," Brian replied, standing up. "Come with me upstairs. I'll tell you about it."

From: "Brian Parker"
To: "Yemiate Bekele"
Subject: Checking On You

What up, friend? It's been a minute. I haven't forgotten about you, but I'm swamped right now. Everything cool with you? Keep your head up. I'll be in touch. Peace.

GENTLE STREAMS poured over Brian's head in the shower, giving him clarity to his thoughts. *Chang can build the website . . . get my man Jaffi to do some promotional posters. It'll read: The Telham Park Benefit Concert is a fundraiser to help third-world— No. Entertainment with unmatched talent to benefit humanity. Nah, I'm not feelin' that. Be a*

part of this exciting movement to build a school in Ethiopia.
See this dynamic show for $20.00. I don't know . . .
something like that. My English teacher can help me out.

Brian chatted with Malyck until midnight about obtaining donations online. He was hungry and restless now and wanted to get out. Walking past his parents' bedroom door, Brian determined his father's snoring at a high level C, which meant he was out for the night. He disarmed the alarm and sneaked out of the house with thoughts of going to Manhattan to see Monet.

Streets on Saturday were lively along the north side of the boulevard. There was a long line of young people waiting to get into The Riva Row Club and cars were double parked for blocks. Brian glanced at the two giggling young women who passed by him as he waited to cross, leaving a residue of smoke mixed with cheap smelling perfume. One of them was wearing tight jeans and platform sandals that she looked uncomfortable walking in. The shorter one had a sexy sassiness to her stride. The two of them together had nothing on Monet.

The owners' son, Mohammed, was making sandwiches in the twenty-four hour bodega and the customer traffic was as busy as any Friday afternoon. "Let me get a roast beef and cheese with everything on it."

"Anything for you," replied Mohammed smiling. He had singled Brian out from the thugs of Telham Park from the first time he'd met him, even before anyone knew he was a computer geek. A friendship ensued when Brian offered to troubleshoot Mohammed's software problems.

Brian substituted a large bag of chips for the French fries. He grabbed two different bags of nuts and a soda and placed them on the counter. When he reached in his pocket for his money, it was empty. He stepped out of the line checking all of them privately sulking. *I know I had wad of singles in my pocket . . . but in my black jeans . . . all the way out here and forgot my money.*

"What's the problem?" Mohammed asked, catching Brian before exiting the store. "My money, yo . . . left it home."

"Wait," he said and called his father who was giving a customer change and said something to him in Arabic. Nodding in agreement he bagged the items and kindly handed it to Brian.

"I'll take care of you later," Brian said relieved, and then suddenly, in bright, bold colors the poster with brown hands stretched out over a coffee field and Ethiopian faces carved in the mountains, created by the Dominican graphic artist at Telham Park High, came alive in his mind and appeared in the window and the store had become a ticketron to the hundreds of patrons that come through there each day. "Ay, when I come back I've got somethin' to ask you."

Mohammed acknowledged his comment with a nod never missing a beat preparing sandwiches.

DAYS BEGAN and ended in a spontaneous fury. Before you knew it the school year was coming to a close. It was a time unlike Brian had ever remembered as the shadow of an uncertain economy loomed; unemployment rising and businesses failing, with no sound predictions of stabilization in sight. People retreated to the simple pleasures of life.

The sun was a circle of bright lights peaking through clouds and smog and when he stared at it, it looked like the moon. And before his very eyes they were spreading wider and multiplying. It was quiet on the school field where he sat after school taking a break from it all. But when he spotted T-Man walking alone he ran over to him.

"Whassup?"

"Dude. What's going on?"

"Where you been?" Brain asked. "I was looking for you."

"Got caught up in some things," he shrugged, looking scared.

Brian positioned himself for the ensuing standoff. "Things like what?"

"Ah . . . a friend of mine asked me to do a favor and I didn't—"

"You rockin' with that porn joint," Brian said, cutting him off. 'That's on you, but my family was wired when the DT's came to my crib."

"It didn't have anything to do with you," he said, backing away. "And I...I didn't know they were gonna—"

"You should've been straight wid me from the door, yo."

"But when I asked you for help, it was just me and this girl havin' some fun."

"That's your business what you do, yo—"

"Then my friends wanted to see them so I told them yeah, for a price."

"All that chatter to me is traceable, yo. And you doin' this with some girl that's only fourteen. That's illegal!"

"I wasn't tryin' to hurt nobody. It was my little hustle and Raheem told me you knew how to make it work."

Nobody could pretend to be that stupid so Brian knew he was telling the truth. "You can't contact me anymore, ya heard?"

"Nah, nah I won't."

"So your boys hittin' you off for some porn action . . . so you must be loaded."

"Nah . . . not really."

Brian never believed a hustler. "So where's my commission since I turned you on?"

"I . . . I don't really have—"

"Why don't you take a couple of these off my hands?" Brian asked, pulling out the stack of tickets he carried.

"What are these?" he asked, squinting to read the print.

"Tickets for a fundraiser. I'm trying to build a school in Africa, and I'm puttin' on a show."

"Word?"

"It's coming up in two weeks."

His eyes brightened, as if he had just received some good news. "Sure, I'll support you. What are they going for?"

"Twenty dollars and I have to sell five hundred."

"That's a lot of tickets to move, yo."

"That's right, so why don't you take some off my hands. Buy five and bring some of your friends?"

Mario whipped out a thin wallet from his right pocket and doled out forty-two dollars. Out of his left pocket came eighty more dollars. Altogether he handed over one hundred and twenty two dollars. "Keep the change," he told Brian. "My contribution to the cause."

Brian laughed all the way home, remembering the words of a music mogul whose autobiography he'd read. He said something to the effect that the people in life that cross you will become your loyal servants in the end. This wasn't exactly the scenario, but it was close enough.

twelve

*B*rian was using a flipper to hit the puck and with every attempt, its collision into the wall sent it flying in directions at high speed. He hit the puck repeatedly only to receive more resistance and finally threw the flipper away. Out of his angry hand he flung it hard and it whirled high in the sky and over a mountain. He chased it only to find himself in a massive sweltering field with cornstalks as tall as trees. The soil felt wet and soggy and a cauliflower path, that had no earthly business there, led him to the bluest lake he'd ever seen.

The phone rang early on Saturday morning and woke Brian out of his virtual hockey dream. He jumped out of bed thinking he had overslept and spun into action. At

6:59am, the sun was shining brightly and the chapel bells of St. Augustine rang beneath the sound of his father's throaty voice.

Brian walked out of his room as tidy as his thoughts. Twenty-two pounds lighter, muscular, well groomed and feeling good, he headed downstairs for his morning workout while mentally running off his checklist. *Suit bag ready, got my hat, tickets for the door, my organizer, the safety box for the cash collection, my camera and gotta have my phone.*

"Where you goin', Dad?" Brian asked, entering the kitchen beaming with sunshine.

Mr. Parker was downing a cup of coffee dressed in a suit and tie. "Auditors showed up at the bank this morning. I've got to go in."

"What! You gonna be there all day 'cause there's still a lot of—"

"Hard to say say right now. Won't know that until the time comes." Mr. Parker wore a concerned look about him swallowing big gulps at a time. "Think you'll be able to handle everything?"

"I . . . I guess," Brian replied, bombarded with a whirlwind of thoughts. "I'ma have to."

"Your mother can help you with anything you need," he said and snatched his keys off the counter. "I'll call you later."

Brian dismissed his feelings of abandonment, but questioned the unpredictability of life. Of all the Saturdays in the world, his father would be called in to work on this one. He built up his hopes in his morning workout thinking of all the things that had to be done between the endless phone calls. Mrs. Parker helped him, reviewing each and every detail down to the eighty-six tickets that were left to sell.

FROM THE door to the stage, every inch of the Horizon Theatre was immaculate. Not a speck of litter anywhere. Inspecting the bathrooms, Brian found they were spotless and smelled good. Christopher and Deshon had been there early managing the volunteer crew and had performed an outstanding job.

Five extra hands had been commissioned to help organize the giveaway goodies around the circular counter, formally operating as the popcorn station. Compliments of his father's network of sponsors; water, soda, chips and a variety of snacks had been donated in massive quantities.

Deshon was assisted by four young men placing the smooth surface runway in position from the elevated stage. His carpentry skills had been at work for weeks putting the piece together and he had begun hammering away securing it in place when Brian was distracted by the incoming call.

"What do you mean the next bus isn't coming until . . . when?" Brian asked, pacing the floor. He was talking to the DJ. "It's gonna take you two hours just to get here. And that's if you don't run into traffic. I don't believe this!"

"What happened?" asked Christopher. He and Country were unloading the industrial fans they had rented.

"Tommy's van broke down in Jersey and they're waiting for a tow truck," Brian explained.

"What are they doing in Jersey?" Christopher asked.

"They did the after party in Ramden last night."

Christopher looked at his watch. "That's a little distance."

"They gonna make it?" asked Country.

"I don't know," Brian nodded. "This is crazy," he said and hung up. "The next bus isn't coming for hours and it doesn't have the room to transport all that equipment, anyway. He said he made some calls but if his cousin doesn't come through, we're hit."

"Think positive," said Christopher. We still have a few hours. Everything's under control here, we're just waiting on the chairs."

The chairs. Where are they? Brian thought. It was Maverick's responsibility to make sure they had arrived on time.

Brian searched his organizer, pulled out the receipt and called the company. "The contract here says customer pick-up. That means you're responsible for transporting them to your destination and bringing them back," explained the owner of Chairs for Affairs. Upon hearing those words, Brian's heart dropped.

"No, he was supposed to have you deliver them here."

"That wasn't the agreement. Read the contract."

"Okay, look, I'm in Telham Park, can you deliver today?"

"I could've, yeah, if I had enough time, but you got five hundred chairs here and our truck's gone for the day."

"No!" Brian objected, stung by his words. "But I'm doing a show here tonight."

"What can I do? We're closing in an hour. I wish I—"

"Kill the noise!" Brian yelled, as the hammering had become so loud it was difficult to hear what the man was saying. "Yo, I said I'm talking!"

Everybody stopped cold.

"I'm sorry, what was that again . . . and there's no way possible for you to make that delivery . . . Lemme call you back. What's your name again . . . alright." Brian ended the call with pins and needles pricking his insides. He pulled at the back of his neck and looked up nodding in disbelief. *This is not happening. We don't have the chairs. The DJ's won't make it here in time. Everybody's gonna want their money back. My father's gonna kill me!*

Brian had delegated the responsibility of the chairs to Maverick after he had sold thirty tickets. The money he made was enough money to cover the remaining costs of the rental and it had been his job to physically go there and make the final arrangements. In Brian's extensive list of things to do, he hadn't bothered with a follow-up to be sure his sometimes not-so-reliable peer was on point. But what could possibly go wrong with a money exchange and an address for delivery.

"What's going on?" Christopher asked. Country was with him. At the same time Monet arrived, sensing trouble in the sudden quiet.

"What's the matter?" she asked.

Nervously glancing about Brian was scared, as vulnerable as a child. "We don't have any chairs."

"What do you mean," Monet gasped, her eyes widened in surprise. "What happened?"

Brian's gaze trailed into the distance. He wanted to explain but no words came out. He wanted to express how scared he was and how rattled his insides were now that his plans had gone awry.

"I don't believe he did this," Brian mumbled pacing about. "I'm gonna look like a fool." Checking his watch again, two more minutes had passed. The hammering resumed.

"You're not telling me anything," Monet said, following him into the lobby, Christopher and Country in tow. "What happened to the chairs?"

In the mix of all the busy preparation, where volunteers were moving in haste, stood Maverick eating a candy bar and bobbing his head to his iPod like it was just an ordinary day. Brian approached him angrily and shoved him into the wall.

"Brian!" shouted Monet. "What are you doing?"

"You were supposed to take care of this!"

"Cool it," Country urged as he and Christopher pulled him away.

"Take care of what?" Maverick asked, startled. "Whatchu talkin' about?"

"The chairs were supposed to be here by noon!"

"I know," he replied. "I took care of it."

"You fouled up is what you did!" exclaimed Brian, shoving the receipt in his face. "Five hundred chairs. We don't have them and they're already paid for!"

The volunteers slowed to a stop; everyone curious about what was happening.

Maverick examined the receipt still confused. "I paid them the money."

"But they were supposed to be delivered. You told them it was a customer pick-up."

"Yeah, this way they'll pick them up for the customer."

"That's not what it means!" Brian protested. "Customer pick-up means just what it says. The customer picks them up. And it's too late to have the company deliver them. They're closing in an hour." Infuriated, Brian kicked the box of balloons and drove his fist into the wall. "Everybody stop. The show is off!"

All the volunteers swooped glances and the word spread quickly. All the hammering and drilling on the stage ceased.

"Whassup," Deshon asked.

"This idiot over here messed up on the delivery. We don't have any chairs and I already paid for them!"

"We can pick 'em up," Alonzo offered.

"In what? You talkin' five hundred chairs."

"Whoa!" Deshon was taken aback, realizing the space and the muscle a delivery like that would entail.

"And the place closes in an hour," Brain told them. "So even if we could get a truck, there's not enough time."

"Where are they?" asked Christopher.

"On the west side."

"If Tommy was here we could have used their truck," said one of the volunteers.

"That's still not big enough," Alonzo voiced. "For five hundred chairs."

"I don't believe this," Brian lamented. *All this work, all this planning.* Brian wanted to cry.

An uncomfortable silence ensued and the squealing door was a welcomed reprieve to the tense environment. No one appeared at first. Seconds later Gilroy entered carrying his horn. All eyes fell on him, the limp in his uneven stride now evident.

"Don't say anything," Christopher said out to everyone and proceeded to meet Gilroy halfway. Then suddenly the room went black. "What the—"

There were gasps, followed by a screeching sound.

"Dee," Christopher called. "Whassup!"

"You turned off the lights?" Brian asked.

"That's not me," he replied.

"Open the door," someone said.

The light from outside poured in the lobby as the door swung out and soon everyone was filing outside.

"I see you met Murphy," said Gilroy.

Befuddled, Christopher asked, "Whose that?"

"Murphy's the law that says whatever can go wrong *will* go wrong."

OUTSIDE, CHRISTOPHER and Country summoned everybody away from inquiring pedestrians. It was a pretty, crisp day. Just then Princess and Nadira jumped out of a car loaded with bags. The panic grew contagious as Monet apprised the girls of what had transpired.

"We've got five hours and thirty seven minutes to pull this show off and we can't give in to obstacles," coached Christopher. Thinking while talking he made a call, seeing himself at the end, a winner, in the same way he thought when making it to the finish line in a track competition.

"It's the circuit breaker," Deshon reported carrying two big flashlights.

"What does that mean?" asked Nadira.

"Too much energy. Keeps tripping the circuit."

"Can't we get Reverend Monday to fix it?" asked Alonzo. "He said he'd be back around 2:30."

"Unless he's got the skills to fix it, he'll have to call the electric company," said Deshon.

"That would leave us four and a half hours to get it working," said Christopher. "It's possible."

Brian could feel his palms sweating and his pulse racing as he nervously drove his hands into his pockets. He began to feel lightheaded by the ensuing disaster and remembered he had only drank water that morning—about six cups. But now, his stomach was filled with anxiety. He arched his back to try to relieve the pressure, but only felt worse. "We're hit!" Brian spewed angrily. "I've got to give everybody their money back!"

"You're not gonna have to do that," Christopher argued, refusing any thoughts of defeat.

Binding the spine-chilling thoughts of a failed project wasn't easy. Images of long lines of anxious spectators, screaming disgruntled ones demanding a return of their money, confusion and mayhem, not to mention the idiot he would appear to be in the community, haunted him. A chill swept over Brian as he walked back inside the dark theatre. It was chaotic in the inner city of his soul, but quiet where he stood.

God help me. This is for Yemi. You told me to do this and it's a good thing so work it out for me, please!

Brian turned on the flashlight and reached for his phone. "Call me as soon as you get this message, Dad. It's urgent! Everything's jacked up. The company can't deliver the chairs. The DJs stuck in New Jersey and the power just went out. There's no electricity, no lights. Call me."

Brian relieved himself in the men's room and returned to the sidewalk composed.

"Gilroy's expecting to play tonight and you don't see him crying," Christopher said, breaking the silence.

"You think people are gonna watch a show with no music, standing up, in the dark?" asked Brian.

"Five hours and thirty one minutes," Alonzo announced.

Monet hastily turned away from the group and began talking on her cell phone.

"Ay, look here," said Country, who was rarely without his barber cape. "I cut too many heads last night, everybody tryin' to look good for this show and I'm missin' out on some customers right now to be here wit'chall, so we betta do su'um. Call the electric company."

Christopher looked at Deshon. "Do they come out on the weekends?"

"On a Saturday, it's got to be an emergency, unless you made an—"

"This is an emergency," Brian urged.

"Not to the electric company," Alonzo argued. "Nobody lives here."

"Call 'em anyway and see what they say," ordered Christopher, "and Brian, you reach out to Reverend Monday to see if he can get back here right away."

"Mr. Hayes does electrical work," offered Maverick.

"Who?" Everyone chorused.

"Mr. Hayes. He lives next door to me."

"You know his number?" Christopher asked.

"No."

"Well get to calling which ya feet," urged Alonzo.

"Huh?"

"Run over there and knock on his door! "Alonzo demanded. "See if he can help us."

Deshon exhaled heavily shaking his head. "Dude is simple, yo . . . and dangerous. That's why you don't— "

"What's the address?" Monet nudged Brian desperately. "The address . . . where the chairs are?"

"Umm . . . Eleventh. Eleventh Street and West Port."

"Can you get there?" They heard Monet ask.

"Okay . . . and you know how to get here, right? . . . Call me." Fumbling excitedly she closed the call and blurted out, "Joel's gonna pick up the chairs!"

"That's what I'm talkin' 'bout!" hailed Country, setting off a surge of energy.

"Remember the guy you helped unload the food truck at the church the other day?" Monet asked.

Brian's brain was in overload and he barely nodded.

"I thought about him and called the church to see if he was still there 'cause he comes in early on Saturday. I told him what happened and asked him to pick up the chairs. He said yes! Yes! He's only ten minutes away from the place so call them and let them know he's coming."

"Now? He's going there now?" Brian asked.

"There you go!" Christopher hailed triumphantly.

"Keep your eyes on the prize," said Country smacking hands with Alonzo. "Ain't over till the fat lady sings. Or in this case, it will be over if somebody don't start singin'."

Only the celebration was far too premature for Brian. "We still gotta get these lights on," he said, holding strong to his worry, "and the DJ."

Flashlights. That's what Brian and the boys used to lead the path into the dressing room behind the stage. Nadira and Princess had made a quick trip to a nearby ninety-nine cents store and picked up several glassed candles. Using them, the room had enough light to maneuver and reflections in the mirror were clear and accurate.

"IT SMELLS good in here," said Alonzo. Brian, Christopher and Deshon, Country, Ricky and Gilroy entered the dressing room with Khalid and Jeremy drenched with sweat. The Urban Violins had exchanged their sound check and warm up time for handy work. It took thirteen hands to set up five hundred chairs in the theatre and the job was complete in no time. Outside, the line had begun to form with excited spectators who arrived early to purchase tickets at the door.

"You guys did good," Nadira commended, offering each of them sheets from the paper towel roll.

"Hand sanitizer is over there," directed Princess. "Help yourself to the food."

Platters of delicious appetizers were all over the dressing room. They had been delivered earlier by Mrs. Parker and several mothers in the neighborhood.

"Any word on the lights?" asked Monet.

"Reverend Monday's out there with some guys now," replied Brian, whose optimism was starting to fade as the hour drew close.

"And that guy Maverick was talking about is out there, too," added Alonzo.

"He wasn't coming back without him," said Christopher, wiping his perspiring forehead. Then he started laughing thinking about the look on Maverick's face when Brian grabbed him. "I thought we were gonna have to bury that dude the way you was lookin'," he said attempting to lighten the growing tension.

"Walked all up his front and down his back," said Country joining in the laughter, and then noticing the smudge on his T-shirt from the reflection in the mirror. "Double the number of these candles y'all got in here, you can light up this room."

"If only you could light up the stage that way, we'd be cool," remarked Alonzo.

The candles had been burning in the room for a few hours and the flames were still healthy and bright. "Where'd you get these candles from?" Deshon asked Nadira.

"Loman's," she replied.

"Did they have a lot of them?"

"They had a few. Want me to go get some more?"

"Yeah, so we'll be sittin' in the light back here when it's dark out there," mumbled Brian who was beginning to pace. "So what's more candles gonna do?"

"It lights up the church at weddings," said Deshon.

"Sure does," agreed Country.

"If we could get enough of them, we could light up the stage," Deshon said. "Just in case the power doesn't show up. That's how they used to determine how much light was needed to brighten up a space when they were building something back in the day . . . by the number of candles burning."

"Listen to the architect," said Country.

"You know how many candles we would have to buy? The store might not have enough," said Alonzo.

"Go to all the ninety nine cents stores," said Deshon. "There's three or four of them open now."

"Wait a minute," said Brian. "We would still have to get people seated."

"The theatre is dark when you're watching a movie," said Country.

"That's real," agreed Christopher.

"If you can light up the stage, around the piano, you can pull it off," suggested Alonzo.

"And we can buy more flashlights for the ushers to use to seat the people," added Deshon. "And tell them to keep them turned on so you can get all the streams of light bouncing all over the place."

Brian's vibrating phone alerted him to a text message. It was Mr. Parker.

**I'm outside with Reverend Monday
and Security.**

At 5:10pm, they were the most beautiful words he had heard all day. "Let me get an OK from my father on this," he told the group. "He's here."

"WE GOT extra batteries and some more flashlights," Jordan said, entering the dressing room. The volunteer trailing him was carrying an arrangement of flowers donated from the local florist.

"Those are beautiful," Monet said. The fragrance wafted through the tense air.

"Channel 8 is here," announced Alonzo, panting with excitement. "I saw him . . . what's that dude's name?"

"Who?" Nadira asked, admiring Kenya's outfit.

"The tall brother, you know the light-skinned one that comes on the news in the morning."

"Morley Dupree?" asked Monet.

"Yeah, him."

"You lyin'!" Nadira exclaimed.

Kenya turned sharply gasping, "Oh-my-God!"

Brian was a ball of nerves, hardly able to tell his left foot from his right.

"The lights," Monet inquired, wiping a stream of perspiration off his face. "He's gonna walk into darkness and—"

"The lights in the lobby and the bathrooms are working off the generator," Deshon explained and dashed back out of the door with a hammer in his hand.

"Yo, it's mad people on the line out there," said Alonzo entering the room.

"We gotta get rolling," said Nadira pacing nervously. "How much time we have?"

"Technically, twenty-nine minutes before doors open."

"Go out there and talk," Brian instructed Jordan feeling hopeful. "Raul can use his video camera to light you up on stage. Kenya can come behind you, play the piano and sing a song."

"And then let Gilroy follow her," suggested Christopher.

"That'll work," Alonzo said and everyone nodded in agreement. "By the time—"

"Hold it, wait a minute," Nadira broke in, hailing a time out. "The last thing we want is to have people talking about how disorganized we were. We need to at least look like we know what we're doing. Okay, let Jordan go out there and entertain the audience while the ushers seat everybody. Make them feel at home. Jump off the stage, shake some hands, kiss a few shorties, ask some questions. You know how to do it," she said eyeing Jordan "and then Raul can follow you with the light. They'll think you're doin' a video or somethin', which actually might be a good thing.

Then formally open up the show, good evening ladies and gentleman, yadda, yadda, yadda. THEN introduce Kenya to sing The Black National Anthem 'cause she can do it acappella. Follow me?"

Everyone agreed including Deshon who had returned.

"Close the curtain. Entertain them for a minute, then introduce Gilroy. The man and his horn don't need any music. You want to sit or stand?" she turned to Gilroy and asked.

"I'll sit."

"Okay, so while Jordan's talking, Deshon will bring out the stool and set up the mike behind the curtain."

"And don't forget I have the smoke machine," Deshon reminded them, "it works with batteries."

"Great!" shrieked Nadira.

"What's going on?" asked Brianna, now entering the room with her models. "Why's it so dark everywhere?"

"Sssh! Give me a second," said Nadira.

Brian was glad to see Brianna and made room for all of them entering the tight space.

"Okay," Nadira continued, "one issue at a time. We've got Jordan first, Kenya, Gilroy and the Twin Violins."

"Walking Poetry," suggested Ricky. "They don't need any music."

"But Makella and her dancers should be the first act after Kenya," suggested Raul. "We're doing a show for a school in Ethiopia, so let's warm 'em up with some Africa. And they don't need music. They've got drums."

"Cookin' with some grease," Country said.

"Yeah, yeah," everyone chorused.

"Okay, okay." Nadira asked reviewing the revised program. After the anthem let Jordan come back and introduce her as a performer, then open the curtains and it'll all be lit up with candles too."

"How long can they last?" asked Raul.

"In the glass they'll burn forever," Monet replied.

"And it won't be a hazard," Deshon added.

"Put the flowers on top of the piano and make it look elegant like they do at the concerts," said Monet.

"But it's in a basket," Princess reminded her.

"Cover it up with some satin or a nice piece of fabric," said Nadira. "I can get my mother to bring us something."

"Let's do this," said Deshon. "And hope the lights come back on soon."

"And what if they don't?" somebody said.

Brian was scared. "We gotta start. But they gonna know that—"

"Nobody knows anything," interjected Mr. Parker making a pit stop to grab something in his tool bag. "And we gotta work this like it was all a part of the plan. Just think positive . . . and keep the snacks coming."

"But Dad, it's gonna be dark soon."

"We'll deal with that when it comes," he said and headed back out.

"FORTY TWO, forty three, sixteen more to light," Deshon announced in the glowing brilliance. He calculated fifty-nine evenly spaced glass candles to sufficiently light up the stage. And then he looked out over the seating area. Slanted streams of light shot across the theatre providing reasonable visibility and with an imaginary eye he could see it filled to capacity.

"Get ready Jordan," said Deshon returning to the dressing room.

Vivacious colors shot across the softly lit dressing room; everyone preparing to get ready.

"Testing, testing," boomed the voice of Alonzo startling everyone. "I got the wireless joints."

"I'ma let you live," joshed Brian, thankful that his friend came through. He was able to borrow several microphones from a family friend that owned a reception hall.

"And look," he said, pulling out an additional one from behind his back. "I got another one, yo." In total there were four microphones.

"Tickets are sold out," Christopher reported, causing a stir in the dressing room. "Ay listen to this," he said, leaning into Brian. "Security was closing the door and somebody's yelling my name, right. It's Akil and he's with Corey and it came to me. They can do that tap dance thing without music . . . and they're good. They didn't have their shoes on so I told him to go and get them 'cause we might need them to perform. I told the security guys they were talent so when they come back, let 'em in."

"That's whassup!"

"Excuse me, hello everyone," interrupted Kenya, calling the crowd of talent to attention in the busy dressing room. She had undergone a make-up and wardrobe transformation and now appeared as the dashing diva.

"Shush everybody!" shouted Nadira. "Kenya wants to say something."

"Okay, I want you to know that you all look beautiful."

"And so do you," said one of the boys.

"Thanks," she giggled. "I know it's been a hectic day, which is not really surprising 'cause the darkest hour always comes right before daylight. So before we go out there I think we should have a moment of prayer . . .

We want to first thank God for inspiring Brian to take on this *incredible* mission to build a school in Ethiopia." The group exploded in applause, catching Brian off guard. The accolade came far too soon as the question of the show's success loomed large. He faked a smile and swallowed against the emotional knot rising in his throat while acknowledging the group through a gesture of hand waving.

"We're with you, Brian," said Kenya "and we're going to do our best, with God's help, to put on a great show, and in spite of the unexpected mishaps, the show's going to be a success, right?"

The group replied in a round of cheers.

"Let us bow our heads for a moment of prayer."

BEHIND THE curtains, Princess and Nadira watched Kenya in awe as her gifted hands flew up and down the keyboard performing several popular songs, welcoming the audience into the theatre. And with the skill of a trained virtuoso, she tickled the ivory keys to lower its volume giving Jordan the cue to begin the show.

thirteen

"**G**ood Evening Ladies and Gentlemen. We welcome you to an evening under candlelight here at the Horizon Theatre. [Applause] I'm Jordan Nichols, your host for the Teens Building A School in Ethiopia Benefit Concert. [Applause]

"I'm gonna step out on a limb here tonight and assume that everyone in this audience can read . . . Uh oh, right . . . it got real quiet up in here. Could be a few closet ill-iterates out there. [Audience laughs] But you wanna hear something that's not so funny, seriously . . . between you and me of course. I don't know a city in America that's fully literate, and this is in the land of opportunity, so don't feel bad if you're out there. But it's far worse, of course, in foreign countries and abroad. In Ethiopia, for example, the adult literacy rate is 36 percent. That's almost 1 out of every 3 people. How well could you function in this world if you couldn't read? Ever thought about it? How about this? Almost 16,000 children die everyday from some hungry related illness. That's one child every five seconds. Almost a million people across the universe . . . hungry! Gotta eat if you want to learn. That's what this evening is all about . . . reaching out across the globe to our brethren in need. [Applause]

"Ladies and Gentleman, let us all stand . . . Here to commence the Teens Building A School in Ethiopia Benefit Concert, singing the Black National Anthem is Telham Parks' R&B vocalist, the lovely, the exquisitely talented . . . Kenya Robinson. [Applause]"

Burgundy curtains sashayed open to a luminous display of evenly arranged tiny torches that captured the elegant songstress appearing out of a fog.

"Lift every voice and sing
Till earth and heaven ring
Ring with the harmony
Of Liberty . . ."

A flood of sumptuous sound emanated from the usually mild young woman. Kenya sang brilliantly, phrasing the words with optimum precision at a steady and even pace.

"Let our rejoicing rise . . ."

Unleashing the power of her extraordinary, multi-octave range, she held the note until it filled every inch of the theatre and then cruised to the end of the verse, holding every ear captive.

"High as the listening skies.
Let it resound loud as the rolling sea . . ."

And through the second and third verse came the lyrical protests to the Jim Crow laws of the twenty century, when the song was first written. Now, almost a hundred years later, the words resonating in the hearts of a new generation, in a new time, still yearning for economic equality, crying against injustice and racism.

"WHAT'S IT looking like, Dad?" Brian asked in the electric atmosphere, catching a glimpse of Maverick who vanished suddenly.

"They called in a specialist."

"From where?"

"The guy Steve, uh Mr. Hayes, he knew about one of those 24/7 operations."

"Who, the one Maverick bought in?"

"Yes."

"Is he any good?" Brian asked anxiously, now realizing that Maverick was deliberately trying to make himself scarce. "Can he fix them?"

"If it's a circuit breaker, there's some hope. If it's something more technical, we're in the dark."

FOLLOWING THE flawless finish, the applause extended beyond Kenya's departure and picked up greater momentum in the dressing room filled with cheering supporters, many of the girls crying at the sensational performance. The kickoff to the concert could not have been more magnificently staged.

"LADIES AND GENTLEMAN, we thought it would be appropriate to begin tonight's concert with a traditional celebration of African rhythm and dance. Are you ready?" Jordan asked beneath the deep rumbling of earthy drums. [Yeah] Don't sound like it to me. Let me hear it again. Are you ready? [Yeah] Now that's what I'm talking about. Please welcome to the stage Makilee's Homeland Dance and Drum Ensemble." [Applause]

In a fusion of beauty eight black females burst onto the stage gliding and shuffling by the rhythms of thundering drums. Robed in colorful cloth they were agile and swift, spreading their arms widely as wings, their feminine movement exploding outward from the hip.

Transitioning to a flat-footed motion they stamped the floor and clicked their ankle shell bracelets, a sacred act regarded as a celebration of the union between man and earth. The audience responded and grooved with it. The intensified drumming instructed the choreography in a blaze of rhythm alternating from the musicians' sticks to their hands. Dark bodies shimmered into a basic two-step, repeating it over and over again. The drama intensified with combination dancing infused with a stream of energy summoned by the drums.

Backstage Nadira and Princess danced to their invented two-stepping, rump shaking, hand flinging moves.

"I'm converting," announced Alonzo, returning to the dressing room with Christopher, Ricky and Deshon. They watched the early part of the performance from the empty balcony where the men were working on the lights.

"Converting to what?" Brian asked.

"To whatever they are in Africa," Alonzo replied. "And find me one like shorty over there."

"You talkin' bout the little one in the front with the big, bright eyes?" asked Christopher.

"Nah, the sexy chocolate one that got them big cantaloupes."

"You mean watermelons," said Country, coming in behind them in a change of clothes.

"Your flavor, too?" asked Deshon.

"I ain't gonna kid you," Country shrugged. "I like 'em meaty. Man can't live off of stringbeans."

Brian found himself laughing for the first time today.

"BEFORE I introduce our next guest, let me . . . let me brief you on his bio. This young brother came from Jamaica only six years ago with a secondhand horn and a dream. He practices more hours than you and I sleep. He attends Washington School of the Arts and was chosen to play with Ray Fields at Central City's Jazz Fest this past spring,

Krowell's Point Symphony Orchestra last summer, and recently a featured soloist in Toliver's Band, just to name a few. Won't you help me welcome the maestro with his horn …Give it up for Gilroy Harkins." [Applause]

Standing at unflinching attention, explosive militaristic fanfare of the old marching bands spewed out of Gilroy's horn in a clear, full tone as the curtains slowly parted. Then he stopped abruptly. He turned his back to the audience and paused before spinning around to reveal a different look wearing a pair of cool Ray Band Sunglasses and began to play an emotionally composed solo of cool jazz. The audience broke into applause.

"He always delivers," said Christopher watching from back stage with Deshon, who was releasing smoke out of the fog machine creating the feel of the jazz cellars of yesteryear.

"He's a cool dude," said Deshon.

"Wait till you hear him blow."

"I thought I saw a light flickering back there," said Country, joining them backstage.

"That's probably Dupree's light you saw," said Deshon. "He had two different camera men with him."

"You gonna talk to him?" asked Christopher.

Brian looked clueless. "I don't know. My father's handling that."

"That reporter's here from The Telham Ledger," Country added. "That Walker dude."

"You jokin'?"

"Everybody's out there," said Christopher. "Except you."

"Listen to that," said Country. The soulful sound of New Orleans had come to Telham Park.

In a gorgeous tone, Gilroy breathed new life into the brass horn with his interpretation of rhythmic improvisation. The group of them launched forward bending to get an ear full.

"Keep him out there," said Christopher watching the contented audience. "He's a concert all by himself."

"You can tell we're from the same tribe," noted Country, referring to his style of changing melodies.

"Playing like that'll make a man forget his blues," said Christopher.

In Maverick's atonement, he shadowed the working crew and offered assistance to anyone in need. Just then he passed by the group handing out bottles of water.

"Want one?" he asked Brian.

"Yeah," he replied anticipating the cool drink to quench his thirst.

GILROY HAD the X factor and everyone loved him immediately. Fireworks ignited from his meaty improvisations calling full attention to his musical ingenuity. One man and his trumpet virtuosity sailed through a maze of styles from the bent-note melody of the Blues, to Jazz, and Country tempered with contemporary R&B. And Gilroy spoke a monologue in between, demonstrating the progressive history of music and how it had been used as a form of communication.

The great performance had brought some relief for the boys returning to the dressing room snacking on chicken wings, Jamaican patties, and codfish cakes.

"What's the temperature out there?" asked Brian who was still wondering how long they would go on before the roof caved in on them or something unexpectedly happen to bring the show to a crashing halt.

"It's not bad," replied Alonzo. "The place is still cool."

"As long as everybody sits still, they'll be alright," said one of the female volunteers.

"Without the music, there's no reason to move," Country added.

AT 8:23pm, in the middle of the poetry slam, the DJ and his partner bolted into the side door of the theatre carrying pieces of their equipment. Every available person went for the truck grabbing a load.

"Still no power," Christopher apprised Ty, who had picked them up from New Jersey.

"We have a backup generator?" said Tommy, handing Mr. Parker an amplifier.

"How long will it take for you to set up?" Brian asked his partner named Tory.

"Once we get the speakers up here, not long."

Brian had an idea, told his father, assembled his friends, and summoned Jordan's attention backstage. "When the poets are finished we're gonna close the curtain so the DJ can set up. Entertain them with some jokes or something. Then you tell 'em everybody's gonna get free chips and soda and the ushers will hand them out so they don't start moving around too much. While you're doing that Deshon's gonna light up the runway with more candles and after that I want you to introduce Akil and Corey to tap dance. That'll give us some more time to stall. Got it?"

"Maurice Dupree wants to see you, Brian," Mr. Parker said closing the call on his cell phone and ushering him through the crowd of models getting ready.

"What does he want?"

"An interview probably."

"But I'm not dressed or—"

"Come on," Mr. Parker said, leading Brian to the side stage stairwell and into the aisle. "Just remember, speak properly and respectfully." Beyond the sound of spit firing prose it was almost quiet among the mass of people. "And none of that: 'know what I'm sayin' ' business."

"I know, I know," said Brian, meandering between the standing attendees.

BEHIND THE curtains the DJs moved swiftly flicking switches, plugging in cords, hooking up amplifiers, and positioning speakers with the help of volunteers.

"This is how they live," said Monet, displaying the photographs of the village community in Kirkos, Ethiopia where the proposed school would be built. It was a dressing room filled with girls for the first time.

"Oh my God," cried Nadira. "Look at the baby." The undernourished child was drinking water from a muddy pond.

"We don't know how blessed we really are," Monet added, flipping to the next photograph. "Look at this." A picture showing a group of young orphans, less than seven years of age, sleeping on cardboard in the danger of night emerged and the candle lit room suddenly went quiet.

"And this one," Monet displayed, "Born with AIDS."

The sobering pictures of abject poverty brought Kenya to tears.

"No!" Monet pleaded softly. "I didn't mean to make you cry."

"It's alright," Nadira said, kneeling down and comforting Kenya and then began sobbing herself.

"That's why we're here," said Princess. "All of us . . . together."

"Just think of all the kids that's going get an education because you sang the Black National Anthem," suggested Brianna.

"That's powerful," added Monet. "So you can only be crying tears of joy, Kenya."

"*Lift every voice and sing,*" bellowed one of the girls, "that's what you said out there tonight, Kenya, so come on, *till earth and heaven ring.*" The tuneless warbling snapped everybody out of the emotional moment and when Princess joined in, the other girls followed. In no time the girls were laughing again.

THERE WAS no mistaking the technicians of tap who were dressed in Black. They took to the stage hoofing and stomping slowly down the aisle of candles. Then they greeted each other at the tip of the runway with a hand shake. The two African Americans, who call themselves "Tip for Tap," walked back to the stage and parted leisurely in opposite directions, their sequined armbands glimmering, matching the tails of their fringed shirts. On cue the dynamic duo effortlessly glided across the floor fusing the moonwalk with tap. Their feet appeared not to be moving but the machine gun sound of tap filled the air. The audience applauded wildly. And that was just the beginning.

"YOU THINK it's gonna be on the news tonight?" Brian asked Mr. Parker, grabbing a few bottles of water out of the cooler.

"It might, but he told me they wanted to include it in the community segment they do on Wednesdays."

Mentally critiquing his responses, he glanced at the setup of the merchandise tables and the general appearance of the lobby as they headed backstage. "It was hard to stay focused with everything going on, Dad, but I think—"

"I need to get back down to the basement," said Mr. Parker entering the theatre and then changing his mind and shooting off down the stairs.

There was a burst of applause and Brian paused to watch his friends. Tapping fast and furiously viewers looked on in amazement as the dancing twosome took off into a combination of choreographic routines and improvisations. They hoofed a style of comedy from the 'flying swing outs' influenced by vaudeville to the more contemporary rhythms of urban street and hip-hop.

Standing in the audience, Brian admired the multi-act, singing and dancing musical extravaganza in the vintage theatre turned concert hall. A place once graced by entertaining icons. There were all kinds of people in attendance, young ones, old ones, scholars, parents, teachers, street thugs and policemen, too. Brian exhaled, relieving the tension in the surreal moment. It had been a call to action, beckoned by a familiar stranger from across the globe. Every ticket had been sold, the raffle table—more than sufficiently supported—and T-shirts were dwindling down. The reality was far stranger than fiction.

TIP FOR TAP EXITED to a standing ovation as the DJ made his entrance with a bass thumping blast of the popular single *It's Not Over Yet*. "Ugh, ugh, ugh," Jordan snapped and bopped across the stage waving to the beat. "Now throw your hands in the air and wave 'em like you just don't care. Say Hoooo!"

"Hoooo!" [Audience response]

"Say Ho, Ho!"

"Ho, Ho!" [Audience response]

Jordan gestured a cue to the DJ to lower the volume.

"Just when you thought you've seen it all," he said, running his hand down the back of his head. "Those boys had me back there tryin' to tap. It's not easy," he admitted and then started shuffling with the tap shoes he had gotten from who knows where. [Laughter] "Are they hot or what?"

"Yeah," the audience shouted. [Another round of applause]

"Our next performance, well this happens to be another duo, oh snap. I just realized we got us a *double duo*. Okay, now let me explain somethin' about them. These guys are innovators, Telham Park originals. They took a classical instrument and turned it into a *class act*. Ya feelin' me on that? [Slight Applause] Making headlines up and down the east coast and soon to hit the west coast, won't you help me welcome the remarkable duo . . . The Urban Violins." [Applause]

IN A STUNNING score, Khalid and Jeremy made their introduction with a pair of violins whining in sync, accompanied by hard pounding hip-hop. Commanding in their energy, playing to a single microphone, they performed the classical strings with virtuosity and temperament, thus demystifying the art of integrating genres. With infectious enthusiasm the innovative duo played like one, vigorously and convincingly, communicating to every age group and musical preference. Camera's flashed all over the theatre as the performance brimmed with bravura.

"Urban Violins iz rockin!" praised Alonzo, riding the rhythm with his easy two-step. It was the only move he knew how to do.

"They doin' nay thang," remarked Country. "First time I ever heard 'em live."

"First time?" Christopher asked, surprised.

"Yeah. Think I'm gonna raise the price on cuttin' their heads . . . 'cause they can afford it."

"THIS IS a good look right here. You . . . me . . . us," said Jordan above the sounds of sirens—a special effect signaling the flaming forthcoming act. "And to keep us looking good we want to showcase this up-and-coming artist who happens to be a fashion designer, [Applause] and one of Telham Park's prized possessions. This time I'm going to give up the mike and she'll make her *own* introduction. [Applause] Give it up, y'all!" [Big Applause]

Telham Park's fierce and sassy female models—Black, white, Hispanic and Asian alike—walked the catwalk to the thick, thumping beat of house music, joined in tow by several tall, muscular men. And detailing the denim and T-shirt line was the sultry, sexy voice of Brianna herself. "How ya'll doin' this evenin'?" she asked, making her entrance to the stage wearing ripped jeans, a skinny fit apple-green T-shirt with sparkling stilettos and accessories. The petite designer wore natural twists and flawless make-up hoped earrings and a big smile.

The sporty urban line combined hip-hop with a mix of retro chic. Her colorful creations displayed on hoodies, crew necks, and long-sleeve shirts were funky and revolutionary worn with a variety of shorts and work boots setting off a screaming frenzy of female viewers. Wild applause and sharp whistling followed as the crème de la super sexy girls modeled the unique collection of shirts coordinated with full length skirts, high heeled boots and ultra short hot pants.

THE THRILLING excitement of a successful performance trumped the hot and sticky atmosphere in the dressing room that looked worse than an upscale department store on Black Friday.

"We pulled it off!" exclaimed Monet who had changed into a beautiful white and purple summer dress with silver high heeled ankle strapped sandals. "Can you believe it?"

Thinking of all the work, ticket sales, sleepless nights and then the 11th hour trials, Brian held his head between his hands, staring into the eyes of sweetheart/partner/ supporter and exhaled a triumphant sigh. "It was the fastest two hours of my life," he said smiling, the youthful glow returning to his face as he pecked her on the lips.

"You mean three," Monet said and returned the kiss on his forehead. "Put you're clothes on."

"It's over now; I don't need to change."

"You can't go out there dressed like that!"

"I have to go out there?"

"Yes," everyone chorused.

"CAN WE give them one more act?" Jordan asked bolting through the door under the hailing chants of *Encore! Encore!*" His eyes darted around the room, to The Urban

Violins, Makilee and the dancers. "No we need something now! Send 'em home hungry for more. Kenya, can you do something?" *Encore! Encore!*

"Another song?" she pondered, springing forward. "Does the DJ have um—"

Gilroy muttered something to Kenya and while they were exchanging possibilities Jordan looked for the tap dancers but one of them were missing.

"Encore! Encore! Encore!"

GILROY AND KENYA were the perfect ending to a warm and cozy evening under candlelight. Performing 'The Heart of Hope,' the duo offered a faithful message, in a spirit of solidarity with infectious melodies infused with optimism for all people—Black, White, Hispanic, Asian, rich and poor, young and old.

Gilroy's rhythm was patient and stylish, almost sounding sensual. And Kenya accompanied him with her soft and delicate vocals. When she dropped out, he picked up with the instrumental solo and she rejoined him in a breathtaking finish of the familiar classic.

Leaning into Kenya's microphone, Gilroy left the audience with three parting words. "To be continued." Then he gently kissed the back of Kenya's hand and together they took a final bow to an exploding audience.

"Oh my God!" squealed Brianna. "Now I'm about to cry."

"And they look *so* good together," Nadira whispered to Princess.

"Don't get me started," nudged Princess. "I was thinking the same thing."

"THAT'S A rare blend, ladies and gentleman," extolled Jordan. "MISSION ACCOMPLISHED!" he shouted. "Thank you," he pointed to the audience. "Thank you. And you! . . . And You! . . . And You! Now give it up for the men and women who gave it up for you! [Big Applause] Now hold on people, where you goin'? We're not finished yet . . ."

"Take off your shirt," demanded Monet. She put on Brian's jacket while Nadira snapped the bowtie around his neck.

"My hat," Brian said, reaching for his Kangol as he was rushed out the door.

"Take these shades," said Princess.

"Nah, I don't need them."

"For effect! C'mon, you're a celebrity now," said Nadira.

"Walk out there with me Monet."

"No. You go out there first and I'll follow you."

"C'MON . . . you didn't really think we were gonna let ya'll go without bringing out the talent now, did you?" Jordan asked the well-pleased audience. "Might be some scouts out there, you never know. But ladies and gentlemen . . . uh DJ, can I get a drum roll, please. [Music and Drums] He's the man who had the vision . . . the courage . . . and took to the task to make all of this happen. [Loud Applause] . . . If you want to meet him, here he is. Give up all you got for Telham Park's own . . . Mr. Brian Parker!" [Cheers and Whistles]

Brian walked briskly down the runway waving to the excited crowd of screaming spectators, tipped his hat to flashlights shooting off from all angles, and then walked off in urgent haste. Seconds later he returned accompanied by Monet and the entire crew of talent filed out onto the stage before a wild audience. The group bowed in unison and made an attempt to head backstage.

"Hold up, hold on," said Jordan. "One more thing. I need everybody's attention . . . Just another moment, please. This is really important. We've got a surprise visitor in the house who would like to say something."

Brian was jolted watching the tall, broad shouldered figure approaching the stage and fell into the NBA player's embrace.

"Razi Hamilton, ladies and gentleman. Telham Park's first and finest power forward.

"On behalf of the West Coast Beamers and myself," Razi began, "We want to present this check to Brian Parker for the *Telham Park Teens Building a School in Ethiopia Project* in the amount of five thousand dollars. [Applause] I know you put a lot of hard work into this and a lot of people's lives will be changed. We're proud of you, man."

"Yo, we need to take this show on the road," Christopher urged, as they made their way toward Brian. He walked out to the edge of the runway, the talent in tow, and they bid the supportive audience a good night.

And then suddenly, as if by divine design, bright scoops flickered on one by one flooding the stage with light from above. Incandescent house lights followed behind them illuminating the audience, the seats and the aisles. Then, when fluorescent lighting brightened the wings of the balcony, an onslaught of applause broke out. As if on cue, the DJ fired out on one of the latest hits prompting a collective grove with the audience. And the music played on as the crowd proudly exited the theatre.

fourteen

New York was gradually coming alive in the dawn's growing light when Brian and his father rolled up to RBC studios for a live taping on *The Early Morning Review*. The success of the fundraiser had lingered on for days and Brian had been bombarded by media inquiries, some he even refused. But when the producers of the popular news show called for a live interview, he welcomed the opportunity.

Crowds of people had already accumulated outside yelling and waiving their signs anxiously awaiting the live performance by Jonabart, the new rock sensation. It was a scene Brian had watched on television for years and now he was here.

"Wasn't too painful?" asked David Landers, taking a seat next to Brian on the set. He was the popular guest show host.

"Not at all," Brian chuckled, referring to the light make-up that had been applied to his face.

"Comfortable with the questions?" he asked, checking his watch for the time. There was twelve minutes left before the scheduled broadcast.

"Yes," Brian replied, preoccupied with the illuminated studio. He was fascinated by the dazzling technology and cameras aimed at the colorful living room set. It felt as relaxing on the set as it had in the green room. He expected there would be more hustling and bustling with a lot of commotion. "This place looks bigger on television."

"Clever camera angles," he said. "That's the magic of set design."

"What made you want to go into broadcasting?" asked Brian, looking across from them at the two-person news set.

"My brother actually got me started," he replied, adjusting his microphone. He was a journalist at first and jumped into broadcasting. As I got older—"

Brian's attention was diverted by his father's gesture as the production assistant seated him, but Dave was happy to provide a summary of his humble beginnings and continued talking. Right up until the broadcast, the two of them, laughing and joking, had reversed roles and Brian was doing the interviewing.

"Standby!" the cameraman called out.

Brian relived the event as they watched the interview with Morley Dupree as an introduction to the segment.

[David Landers]

A sixteen-year-old from the Telham Park section of Brooklyn demonstrates how one individual can, in fact, make a difference. Brian Parker, who attends Telham Park High School, organized a community fundraiser with a group of local talent. His goal: To raise $10,000 to build a school in Ethiopia, Africa. Ironically, he came across the idea when, get this, he was on punishment, grounded for being a bad boy. With nothing to do and chatting online, Brian meets sixteen-year-old Yemiate, who had been learning how to use a computer by a missionary group, and the two quickly became friends. Here's Morley Dupree with Brian at the Teens Building A School In Ethiopia Benefit Concert.

Morley: Just over four months ago Brian, you met a young man from Ethiopia on line. So what kind of conversations did you have? I mean, did he come out and ask, "Hey somebody over in America, please build us a school?"

Brian: No. [He chuckles] It started off just like a regular conversation. You know, what's your name, where you from, what's going on . . . like that, ya know. Then we kept in touch . . . like every other day and I started learning things about him, his way of life, his culture. He was learning about mine.

Morley: So tell us what your inspiration was behind building a school?

Brian: Yemi talked about school and education like it was this great big dream or something. Everybody in America goes to school . . . if they want to. But when I learned that children in Ethiopia will walk five miles a day—and that's one way—just for a chance to open a book and learn, I felt like I needed to do something.

Morley: But build a school? That's a serious undertaking.

Brian: It is but when I learned what it costs to build a school I . . . I felt this responsibility. Ten thousand dollars in America is not a huge, huge amount of money. I mean it is for someone like me. But then I talked to some people about it. And when I realized it was feasible to do, I got busy thinking of ways to raise the money.

Morley: Really, you felt that compelled?

Brian: Yeah, I did, and I wanted to get everybody else involved, too. Like my friends, people in the community . . . like a movement.

Morley: What have you learned from this experience?

Brian: Wow . . . the first thing I learned is . . . how fortunate we are living in America. We have all these material extras, things we don't even need. And it makes us lazy. Like when you eat too much and you're too full to move, know what I'm sayin'?

Morley: Yes, I absolutely do.

Brian: We take our education for granted . . . myself included sometimes, I gotta be honest. Yet, in third world countries people would give anything to be able to read, live out there dreams and be successful.

Morley: That's interesting, particularly when you're—".

Brian: Oh, and I also learned never to complain. In America, we have every advantage.

Morley: Okay, so tell me, what would you say to someone your same age that doesn't feel, let's say worthy of anything, or doesn't feel they have anything to contribute to the world.

Brian: . . . I would tell them every human being has something unique about them to give away. Um, it's like your purpose. And that purpose could be feeding someone . . . teaching someone . . . maybe even healing someone. And you don't have to be a celebrity with money or some famous writer or director to do that. It's the little everyday things we do that can lead to big things. Like this school. It'll help hundreds, maybe thousands in the future. So all the hands that came together to make it happen have achieved something really great. Dr. King once said: "I want to be first in generosity." It's not about being big, or perceived as important. "But the greatest among you will be your servant."

Morley: And on those profound words spoken by sixteen year old Brian Parker—sure you're only sixteen?

[Brian laughs]

Brian: Thanks for coming out.

Morley: It's been an honor. Best to you with the show.

[Cut to the Studio]

David: Welcome Brian, good to have you here today. [They shake hands]

Brian: Good to be here.

David: What an encouraging story. Did you ever think you'd accomplish something of this magnitude?

Brian: [He shakes his head] And end up on The Morning Show, never.

David: [He Laughs] You must be some inspiration to your peers. And your parents must be proud.

Brian: Yes . . . they are.

David: Brian, you know so many people were moved by your courage in seeing the *Teens Build a School in Ethiopia Project* come to fruition . . . particularly one individual we've brought here today who wanted to meet you. Turn to your left. Someone by the name of Yemiate is with us via satellite.

"Hello Brian. How are you my friend?"

Brian stared into the face of the young man in wide-eyed astonishment. It was the person he'd known for months through an inanimate, technological tool, and felt an emotional attachment to, and now here personified. He was brown, keen featured, with curly looking hair and a slender build.

"Yemi . . . is that really you?"

"Yes, it is really me."

"You look like a tall dude."

"Yes, I am over six feet tall. And you look real strong."

[Brian is smiling, flattered.]

"I can't believe it," Brian laughed.

"We are so excited over here. When the news came that they were building a school, I didn't believe them. I am still in amazement that you are responsible for this. To you we are grateful."

"Nah, I'm the one that's grateful. You changed everything for me, dude."

"In what way?" Yemi asked.

"Like I feel like I can do things I never did before."

"That is the way we feel," he beamed brightly. "And the school will make everything possible for us. And I have been told that I may be able to visit America one day soon."

"Ah that's cool, man. I can show you those cars I was telling you about."

"We thank God that our prayers have been answered and we send our thanks to you."

"'Hope is the sweetest thing the soul can bare,' remember?"

Yemi breaks a broad smile. "Yes I do and it tastes very good right now."

[Everybody laughs.]

"Good-bye for now, my friend, and thank you again to everyone in America."

"You're welcome, from everyone here. Peace."

"WHEN THE station got word of the story, they reached out to one of their affiliates in Addis Ababa," Mr. Parker explained, seated inside the town car headed back to Telham Park. "A correspondent went out and spoke with the church that's heading the project and he wanted to meet Yemi."

Brian neither smiled nor frowned, but observed the sights of the city. But then the corners of his mouth couldn't resist the urge to grin at the thought of Yemi being picked up from his village and driven in an air conditioned car, given a new shirt and pants to wear and a good meal to eat— hopefully several good meals—and a school in his name. "Incredible," Brian nodded, grappling with the inexplicable series of events. "I didn't see this coming."

"The media's always looking for a good story. A little bit of networking . . . you'd be surprised what you can do. And this is just the beginning."

"Right," Brian agreed, letting his head fall back.

"Acknowledgements and thank you's," muttered Mr. Parker, who was always thinking.

"Huh?" he asked, turning his head sideways.

"You've got to send something to all the people that helped you. Then again, we could put something together at Zaspers. A luncheon . . . maybe a dinner."

"That place is expensive."

"They made it happen for you, show some gratitude. You can afford it."

"I wasn't exactly planning on—"

"It's not about what you planned. It's a cold world out there and when you find people who'll support you, who'll be loyal to you . . . better take care of them."

"You're right," Brian conceded, considering his prospective. He was generous by nature, but of the things he was partial to.

"We've got to set some goals, put together some ideas for fundraisers, and somewhere down the line you'll want to start a non-profit organization."

"How does that work?"

"Establish a company and you register it as a 501(c)(3). You can get more funding that way."

"That'll work."

"But you gotta get serious, working on it 24/7."

"You know me, Dad."

"Yeah, I do. That's why I'm telling you."

Brian chuckled, but was really smiling inside, feeling empowered by what he had achieved. "It's like anything's possible."

"That's right and when people see you making moves, especially for good causes, they wanna help."

"I'm thinking we can raise more money for computers, for books and school supplies . . . and I can get Yemi a cell phone so he can call me and tell me what they need. Then move from village to village building schools."

"Ay . . . the first time you did it; it was a mystery. Second time, you make history."

"That's real, Dad. And maybe we can go to Ethiopia next summer . . . like five of us—Christopher, Deshon, Ricky, and Raul. We could hang out with Yemi and do a video of the trip, come back here and make a documentary out of it. That would be hot!"

"You . . . over there without me?"

"What, you don't trust me?"

Mr. Parker chuckled, looking out at the sea of people as they inched through snarled traffic around Madison Square Garden. "Maybe tomorrow."

The comment went right over Brian's head as his mind was spinning with ideas. "We can even sell the documentary to public schools to raise more money."

Mr. Parker took Brian by his neck smiling and jostled him with pride. "I'm feeling you, dude."

"OKAY, JUST be natural and don't walk out of range," Monet told Brian, adjusting her videocam on the tripod. Then she positioned herself next to Brian holding her cell phone to her ear.

"Haven't I seen you before?" he asked, just as he had done on the first day they'd met.

"You don't look familiar," Monet replied, drawing up a curious frown.

"Yeah, it was a few weeks ago. There was a fire in the train station."

"I remember that," she responded. Smiling, they turned toward the camera pretending to be walking. "And cut." Monet directed. "That's how I want to end it. See, I'll have all this different footage of my father from the past and then today at fifty. Then I'll do like a quick summary with some still shots of him and my mom when they first met and a live shot of them today, thirty-four years later. Then, I'll switch to that shot of us first meeting 'cause they met each other at our same age."

"Oh, that's cool."

"Yeah."

"So does this mean we're headed for marriage?"

Monet fell back in wide-mouthed laugher, her teeth gleaming in a broad smile, as if she were warmed by the idea of sharing her life with Brian. "Only if you promise to keep me laughing until we're old and gray," she uttered sweetly.

"Oh I can make that happen . . . easy."

ABOUT THE AUTHOR

JENNIFER BURTON, a native of New York City, has always been intrigued with multicultural interaction. While teaching in a Brooklyn high school, she became deeply steeped in youth culture, observing their enthusiasm for urban contemporary fiction. Her literary insight, along with her passion for writing, prompted the creation of the Telham Park series. Jennifer resides in New Jersey.